BEACHHEAD
IN
BOHEMIA

BEACHHEAD IN BOHEMIA

Stories by

Willard Marsh

Louisiana State University Press
Baton Rouge

For Joe

and for
Matt, Phyllis,
& Hank

These stories have appeared in the following periodicals:
Denver Quarterly, New Mexico Quarterly, North American Review, Yale Review, Transatlantic Review, Southwest Review, Northwest Review, Esquire, The Carolina Quarterly, and *Rogue.*

Copyright © 1969 by
Louisiana State University Press
Library of Congress Catalog Card Number: 71-86494
SBN Number: 8071-0914-2
Manufactured in the United States of America by
Seeman Printery, Inc., Durham, North Carolina
Designed by Jules B. McKee

CONTENTS

BEACHHEAD IN BOHEMIA

MY HOUSE
IS YOURS

At one time, the Posada Zopilotl marked the last leg of the Camino Real, the tortuous royal highway that had linked Guadalajara with the capital of New Spain. Carriages had been stationed in its courtyard; mule trains and their drivers had endured the democratic night together on straw a foot above the faded carriage ruts; and when the straw was buried by cement a Mercedes-Benz had paused there in its flight to the frontier, bearing a divisional general who, in losing a revolution, lost everything except his honor and a bare half million pesos salvaged from the previous, corrupt regime.

Shortly before the end of the Second World War, the grandniece of a papal count, the Senora Fuentes Villanova y Valdez-Herrera, was approached by the North American Mr. Barnaby Kidd. The senora was a widow tutored in the philosophies of neither commerce nor human frailty. The North American was less handicapped. He had seen how Mexico's tourist trade was mounting through the inaccessibility of Europe and the Orient, and the extent to which the government permitted foreign investment. After an examination of the confused tax structure, Mr. Kidd accordingly assured Sra. Villanova that a more aggressive management of the Posada would redound to their mutual benefit. As a result, four centuries after King Philip's emissaries had crossed themselves as shelter loomed on their horizon, an agnostic ambassador named Jaime Guadalupe Gomez assayed the hospitality of the Posada Zopilotl.

Partly open to the sky, the cool tile patio was strewn with cowhide chairs and plants in massive earthen jars. A magazine rack at the near wall offered visitors the next to latest word from home, running the octave, if it was one, from *Fortune* to *Astounding Stories*. The office behind it cashed traveler's checks (at five centavos discount on the peso), sold souvenir ashtrays (the peon asleep beneath the cactus), authentic costume jewelry, and books on understanding bullfights. From the corner, belligerent in size, volume, and shifting choleric hues, a juke box presented the clientele with its nostalgic native rhythms.

A pair of middle-aged *matrimonios* (the men in lacquered sombreros, their women in silk rebozos) were waiting uncomfortably around a slab stone coffee-table to learn if it was sufficiently past break- fast hour to soothe their hangovers with a tequila collins. They looked up expectantly as Jaime came through, setting themselves for an exchange of pro- nouncements on the lack of excitement. The travel folders had no doubt implied the air was broiling with it.

"Bwaynus deeus," one of the ladies called.

"Good morning," Jaime said cordially.

Animation faded on her face as he continued past. Her husband checked his watch to see if it was run- ning.

How pleasant it must be to be a tourist, Jaime thought. One could stroll the colorfully squalid streets, pitying the people for their lack of imported coffee, cigarettes, and toilet paper, and end up in bed with one another's wives—Northamerican women being un- derstandably promiscuous when their husbands' vigor was unmasked by the few children they were capable of fathering.

The patio led past a corridor awaiting completion. A stack of bricks showed through the gap, along with a wheelbarrow of dried mortar and other evidences of industry. A delicately knuckled file of coffee trees concealed this litter from the garden. They were in pubescent blossom now, and they would yield kilo upon kilo of coffee before they died and were replaced. It was beyond doubt that they would die eventually. Whenever they did, it was beyond doubt the corridor would still need finishing. Until establishments were fully constructed, they weren't fully taxed. Bougainvillea spilled from the mossy walls, wine turning blood through the leaf-broken light. And below stood bottomland where Lake Chapala stood in peak years: swelling its banks through the long plum-heavy rains, withering through drought cycles, returning in tides of its own like a sea with no moon.

Jaime found Mr. Kidd in the dining room. Dressed in the exhibitionistic manner of his personality, in faded shorts and a garish tweed sport coat, he was parrying complaints about the menu. *What's wrong with prunes every day? Good for you, keep your bowels open.* At no time was Jaime introduced to any of the guests, either through deliberate omission or perhaps only the Northamerican impatience with courtesy. When the room finally emptied Kidd took a chair opposite him, deaf to any amenities one might exchange.

Jaime smiled at the smaller man. "I am here, like you know, in the behalf of the Senora Villanova," he began. "She gave to me the authority to discuss some kind of settlement on your lease. She wishes you will give it up now, instead of to wait the little time when it expires. She wishes to make the Posada Zopilotl more—" he hesitated, trying to avoid insult, "—more Mexican in custom. Like it was before."

"You mean bankrupt?" Kidd said.

"At the senora's age, income is not her first wish."

"Yeah? Well, at my age it is."

"Of course. That is why I have come here to discuss with you."

"You want me out, right? And you want me to name my price, right?"

"I have admiration for your directness," Jaime said.

"Okay, Gomez." Pulling a notepad from his pocket, Kidd scrawled a figure on it. "My lease has three little years to run. This is about the profit that I pull each year. Multiply this by three and we'll tear up the paper."

Jaime stared at the notepad. "But this sum is impossible."

Kidd shrugged.

"I could go to the senora with some price of reason, but *this* . . ."

"Sorry. I buy tuberculosis seals at Christmas. That's enough charity for any one year."

Jaime dropped all effort at civility. "This is your final price?"

"Give you a break," Kidd said negligently. "I'll let you have a five percent cash discount."

"In this case, Mr. Kidd, I wish to warn your lease will be annulled by law."

"That's a hot one. On what grounds—or don't you need any in this country?"

Maintaining his temper, Jaime said, "On the grounds of breaking the letter and the spirit of the lease. One, by the immorality of many guests over periods of long

time. The nude bathing of the school teacher in the
Spring of Grace is one example. We have many others.
Two," he said, "by your policy of repulsion to Mexi-
cans for guests."

"Oh, I don't know about that," Kidd said lazily.
"Always a certain amount of high spirits in any vaca-
tion crowd. A lot less than in some Mexican hotels. At
least there's no generals using the back bar for target
practice Saturday nights. And as far as the repulsion of Mexicans goes," he said, "hell, *I* don't repel
them. The prices do." He sat forward angrily. "This
isn't someplace any *pelado* can use the floor for a toilet, shove the customers around, or figure any woman
in the bar's a whore and he can automatically afford
her. They know that from the price list, that's why
they aren't around."

"I was not meaning the uneducated people," Jaime
said, irritated at his own embarrassment. "There are
many Mexicans, like myself, they can pay these prices
for a little visit sometimes—"

"Oh sure, but you're an exception. You've lived
around Americans so long. But even with the upper
class Mexicans—"

"An upper class Mexican would not put feet in the
Posada now," Jaime said bitterly.

Again Kidd shrugged, "Upper middle class, then.
They're almost as bad. They bring their own lunch
and expect free setups. Just one family of them, with
all their table-hopping and their spoiled brats, can
empty the joint in five minutes. Course that seldom

happens here," he added. "A fairly small operation like this one, we're usually booked up way in advance."

Jaime sat in the imminence of defeat, knowing that the bad faith of Barnaby Kidd would be difficult to prove. It would be a drawn-out battle, the problems and expenses as distasteful to the Senora Villanova as the present mismanagement. It was outrageous that one of the republic's greatest natural wonders, Lake Chapala, should be so grossly exploited for the casual entertainment of a few wealthy foreigners, while the decent people of small means who owned it, the *gente decente*, were denied comfortable access to it. Unfortunately, the village could support no more than one first-class posada.

"But I suppose that's the old story," Kidd was saying. "Guy comes down here and gets things going on an efficient basis, and right away you start thinking about expropriation."

Christ in His pain! Jaime thought. "I wish to remind you that your country has a larger history of expropriation than ours. We lost more than the half of all our land to you, in one of the most unjustified wars of history. Very well, this is past. But with other countries—what is the Good Neighbor Policy when a people wish to realize themselves? A brigade of marines! Even in your own boundaries," he said in the excitement he no longer dominated, "the shameful custom of giving encouragement to whole industries —your distilleries, for example, to permit them to invest their capital in plants and taxes—then with one scratch of the pen to make it criminal for their existence! And in the last war, when the Americans of Japanese descent were imprisoned—what about the expropriation of *their* lands?"

"Relax, Gomez," Kidd said easily. "Like you said, the word is history."

"Yes, the American Way," Jaime said, weary now, "to strip the resources to the bone, then move out and leave Mexico to struggle with the consequences. We must grow at our own rate, not yours. The Posada Zopilotl is not the true economy of here. Agriculture, fishing—*that* is the economy. When the artificial one you have built up is gone, how will the people support themselves?"

"Oh, they'll get by," Kidd said evasively, "no one's starving. Anyway, what do you care? You don't live here."

"But of course I do. I was born here, this is my *patria chica,*" Jaime said, with less conviction than he wished. "This was a pleasant little village, here before you came. A family could come out for a week's end to refresh themselves. *Now* what is there? Freaks and deviates of all descriptions."

"Good publicity," Kidd said dryly. "Look, Gomez, you're a big city man, you're a Guadalajara attorney. Your only interest in an Indio village like this is the fee you're pulling down to break my lease."

"This is not so," Jaime said in dignity. "My only fee is sentiment." And it was the truth.

Kidd seemed to realize it. His expression changed
from casual enmity to casual contempt. "Now we're
getting somewhere."

Slowly his fingers formed the classic gesture of the
mordida, the bite: How much will it cost me for you
to forget about me?

Jaime got to his feet stiffly. "My honor is not for
sale, Mr. Kidd. The law is also not for sale. You will
find this out very soon."

"Oh I never knock the laws of Mexico," Kidd said,
quite seriously. "They're probably one of the greatest
set of laws in the world. Trouble is, nobody pays any
attention to them."

"You will find out different very soon. You have my
word." Jaime glanced down at his coffee and reached
for his billfold.

Kidd waved it off. "On the house."

"Thank you."

The coffee had stood untouched, and it was cold,
but he took a polite sip of it before he turned to leave.

Outside, a throng of parasites surrounded him, loud-
ly offering their shoddy souvenirs and services. Jaime
dispersed them with a sweep of his hand. What kind
of trades were these for grown men? Across the street,
he saw that his Chevrolet had been given an unneces-
sary polishing by two children who were waiting for
the owner to appear, the *jefecito*, whom they would
pester till he tipped them. Did Mexico have no voca-
tion of her own except the mastery of swording bulls?

His mood persisted as he started across the plaza. Just then someone hailed him. He turned to see the priest, Padre Rubio, poised as if for a portrait in his somber but fastidiously pressed black suit, his breviary between his delicate fingers. A wan and small-boned man of strict views, he had succeeded the fat, easygoing priest who'd been a childhood favorite of Jaime's.

"How goes it with you, *hijo?*"

"Well, thank you, Padre," Jaime said. "And with you?"

"Less well, unfortunately." The priest smiled. "My office is becoming something of a luxury for Zopilotl. So few people avail themselves of it in these times."

"It is the tourist season. Perhaps they are busy working for the foreigners."

"Perhaps. But I think it is not the work that keeps them from the church. Better said the life they are exposed to of the foreigners. The vistas of such idle sin can be most tempting. They seek to emulate it."

"On a much smaller measure, of course," Jaime smiled.

"Intent is the measure, not degree," the priest reproved.

"Clearly," Jaime said in annoyance.

"They have turned from God, and He has turned from the Lake of Chapala. Why else has it declined so in this past year?"

"Who knows?" Jaime said politely.

The priest shook his head. "And now the influence of the foreigners seeks to extend itself in yet another direction. They are collecting money to enlarge the school a whole grade more. A fifth grade, they envision."

"Do you not like this idea?"

"I am not sure. School as a place to learn to read and cipher, surely. But there must be an end of it in time. If not, the children are great dreaming idlers, when they might be in the fields to earn their honest bread. Well, I burden you with my small troubles," the priest smiled. "What brings you back to Zopilotl, business or a family visit?"

"The two," Jaime said, "conveniently so."

"Your mother will be glad to see you. She prays weekly that you find your way back to the church, *hijo mio.*"

Jaime nodded briefly. There was nothing he could say, and he resented being called "my son" by a man somewhat his junior.

But oddly enough, he could have been in this same priest's position, he reflected as he left the plaza. He had been the first-born, the hope of Guadalupe and Esperanza Gomez. They'd managed to send him through school (it ended at the third grade those days), and then, by a miracle of industry and thrift, to the seminary in Guadalajara. Their faith in him was amply rewarded. He'd been an alert student, eager to learn and quick to challenge. Too quick, it turned out. For his nagging curiosity, cramped by the pious generalities of his confessors, drove him to forbidden books on the *Indexo.* Through these, he'd hoped to resolve certain troubling inconsistencies in dogma he'd discovered. But instead, in the musty bookstalls off of Avenida Juarez, where he came to know the man the avenue was named for, and in adventurous library stacks, in the blazing light of history, Jaime's place in Paradise was lost to him.

He had become an ardent revolutionist, a spy in an enemy embattlement, continuing to receive Communion, contemptuous of God for not striking him dead. His private rosary was the thousand documented proofs that the consistent, verminous hulk in the path of Mexican progress was the Mexican Church. Who owned fully half the land before the Reformation, and owned mortgages on the other half? Who held Her vast funds back when Mexicans were dying in the battlefields of Texas under a dictator She had sponsored? Who rode another dictator into power, perpetuated him for thirty-five years while he gave the country's wealth to foreign interests, and when a savior finally ousted him, applauded the butcheries of the man who murdered and succeeded him? Yes, the Church was always present when Mexicans faced death. Why shouldn't She be? She was responsible for so much of it.

By the time Jaime left the seminary, he had the education and the strength to work his way through law school. And eventually his youthful political intensities were blunted by the growing stability of the government, and by his own growing standard of living. He was no longer a combatant now. But somewhere, he supposed wearily, the battle was still raging for the enlistment of his soul. Occasionally in nightmares he could hear its distant rumble, the adversaries so perfectly matched that he, the double deserter, could change its outcome by the solitary engagement of his convictions. But he had been emptied of such vanities long ago.

Turning into an alley behind the church, Jaime hurried toward the sprawling weathered house that endured at the end of it. He had both the eager anxiousness to see his people and the nervous anxiousness to get it over with and return where he belonged. He threw open the door of the house of his birth. The old sour nostalgia instantly attached itself to the furnishings that sprang to view, so acutely intimate down to the slightest scar, and so irrevocably disconnected from himself.

His sister Paz was sitting, watching nothing. Then she felt Jaime's presence, turned, and recognition slowly filled her eyes.

"*Mano!*" she cried, jumping up and rushing to him. "Where have you been, why do you go away so often?" she babbled as he held her to him. Over her shoulder he saw the tamped dirt floors, hard as tile; the glossy advertisements cut from discarded United States magazines and tacked along the walls. From the ceiling, drab common birds suspended in their drab reed cages, sulking their lives away as furniture until they died and were replaced by new ones that his youngest brother would trap.

"We had baked liver last night and the senor cura

came in afterward and Heriberto Ochoa ran away to Oaxaca . . ."

Paz continued chattering as Jaime smoothed her hair, not listening. She was twenty-five years old, and mentally a child of five. No one would ever marry her, but it didn't matter. She had a plump live bastard baby all her own, who was named Angelito because she was incapable of imagining how she could have gotten him except direct from heaven. Her own name, Paz, meant Peace, and was as suitable.

Now Jamie saw his mother standing in the kitchen doorway. She watched him with an expression in which felicity and sorrow oddly mingled. Detaching himself from Paz, he strode over to her.

"*Mamacita,*" he said gently, and spread his arms.

She came into them, hugging him clumsily and murmuring his name. Her cheek was leathery against his own, her body brittle, bearing the odors of domesticity and erosion.

"Padre Rubio was here last night," she said.

"Paz told me."

"He asks about you often."

Jaime didn't say anything.

"Can you not see him while you're here?"

"I just saw him."

"Truly?" His mother's face brightened.

"We have nothing for each other," Jaime said flatly.

Her face went slack again. "I tell him you are busy in the city, that this is when your fortune must be made," she faltered, "when you are young. Later there will be time for your return to spiritual considerations." Feeling him stiffen she said quickly, "And your wife, she is in good health?"

"Yes, thanks."

"Also the little one, my granddaughter?"

"Also," he smiled. "She waxes fatter every day."

"Why did you not bring them?"

"I had no opportunity," Jaime said uncomfortably, "my trip was unexpected." Actually his wife, who claimed fifty percent Spanish blood, was embarrassed by his family and except on certain inescapable holidays avoided them.

"I should not molest you," his mother said, "you come so seldom even without molestations. And now you must be hungry, after such a long trip."

"With the highway?" Jaime laughed. "There is a highway built from Guadalajara, remember?"

"*No le hace.* One excuse for cooking is as useful as another. Come, Paz, you great lout!" she called. "Let us kill a chicken for the *mole.*"

"Which one?" his sister said eagerly. "The cockerel of the torn comb?"

"Umm, he will be too tough. Better that we take a pullet. The speckle-breasted one has good flesh."

"But is she large enough?"

"I wonder. Perhaps her mother might be better. The useless creature hasn't put an egg all week . . ."

They disappeared out back, then Jaime heard his father being shouted from his hammock to go see who had arrived from the capital of Jalisco. He came in

with his stooped shuffe, blinked, then stood trembling
from either emotion or the full weight of his sixty
years. They met midway in an *abrazo*, and again, as
with his mother, Jaime saw the fine firm lineaments of
youth impending through their mortal mask, like the
echo in a clouded mirror.

His father stepped back, looked him up and down
as if examining a prime horse, put a shy hand to Jaime's
arm to squeeze the strength that had once sprung so
wondrously and unremembered from his loins. Then
in embarrassment he said, "Would you like a *copa*?
There is some pulque in fresh yesterday from Jiquil-
pan."

Old Guadalupe got a covered crock from the rear
room and filled their glasses with the frothy white
liquor of the maguey cactus. A cheap drink, leading
eventually to a cheap drunk, it was sold in rowdy slum
establishments with such names as "Long Live My
Disgrace" and "The Sacking of New York by the Aztecs
in the Year Two Thousand." As always, Jaime experi-
enced the old guilty relish of its sour-acid flavor, knowing that it was no doubt unsanitary and that it would
continue fermenting in his stomach. Then, because it
was of duty rather than of interest he asked, "How
went the last crops?"

His father shook his head sadly. "Less well."

Jaime sighed to himself. For some years now he'd
been seeing to it that his father had produce to plant
on his little hillside plot, and the wages and equipment
to harvest it. Guadalupe would go through the motions

of repaying him in good seasons, skip the poor ones, and Jaime's overall loss was perhaps a couple of thousand pesos a year. Substantially less than his wife spent in her church activities—not that a husband had to justify his own expenditures.

"What happened?" Jaime asked, merely for statistics. "Was it lack of rains?"

"*Pues* no, there were rains enough," Guadalupe said. "More might have been welcome, but the water did not lack."

"What then?"

"It was that tomatoes were the crop, and they were so in abundance no one gained much money."

"Why did you not plant something other than tomatoes, then?"

His father had a vague, embarrassed look. "Everyone was choosing them, so it seemed safest." There was an unvoiced reproach that the eldest son had not been on hand to make such decisions.

They refilled their glasses, both eager to leave the subject. "How fares Nacho at the garage?" his father asked.

"The same," Jaime could answer without lying.

"He will make a good machanic. He is a good boy. Warm-blooded, as I was, but he will get somewhere . . ."

Somewhere like the Tres Marias penitentiary, Jaime thought. He knew, from seeing his younger brother around such luxury bars as the Del Parque and the Fenix, that Nacho was at best a combination tourist guide and gigolo. He'd have the equipment for it, all right. We have good looks in this family, if nothing else.

This was probably because his parents were first cousins (his mother also being a Gomez). When the good genes doubled up the gifts were abundant. But when they came out bad, as in the case of Paz (who would have been a handsome woman if there were any sign of inhabitance behind her eyes), the result was a long succession of baby coffins, beginning with Maria (who would have been the oldest), Domingo, Natividad, the first Nacho, Enrique and Concepcion. Dead at birth, dead of night air, of the fits; of dysentery and a scorpion's sting; of ignorance and bad nutrition, the cura's blessings and the witch woman's balms; dead by God's Will or God's Indifference, and finally not dead at all but safe in heaven now, raised there by debts contracted against next year's harvest, and kept there only by the installments being promptly met.

The sound of whistling cut through his thoughts. Feet came up the alley, the door flew open and Dionisio, Jaime's nearest brother, sauntered in. He lifted his eyebrows in surprise. "Senor *Licenciado*," he said in mock politeness, "Mr. Attorney. What business brings you to the house of Guadalupe Gomez?"

"The business of testing pulque," Jaime said, hiding his irritation. "Serve yourself to some."

"With such distinguished company, how can I refuse?" Dionisio filled a glass from the crock, held it aloft to Guadalupe. "Your health, little father."

Old Guadalupe murmured an acknowledgment, and

the two of them discussed some recent gossip. Listening absently to his brother's vulgarisms, Jaime thought: another Gomez *guapo*, trading his profile for an indolent life with a wealthy alcoholic gringa, the Mrs. Victory Richmond.

Dionisio had been born a year after Jaime, and in early childhood they had been inseparable. Summer evenings they would lie out in the fields, manufacturing visions of becoming toreros together. Afternoons, they would practice passes with a stolen blanket for hours on end. But with Jaime's enrollment in the seminary they grew apart. He would have been insufferable in those days, he supposed, parading his student mannerisms for the approval of his parents and the sullen confusion of his brother. Now, perhaps in self-defense, he had become Jaime's polar opposite.

Smiling at their dozing father, Dionisio said, "He is an old man, this one. Even in the last month he is older."

"*Parece que sí,*" Jaime agreed awkwardly.

"How is your wife, hombre?"

"Ah, my Spanish wife. How is *your* wife?"

"Which one?" Dionisio grinned.

For an instant they seemed on the verge of speech. But the vocabulary for it was too old for resurrection. Murmuring something about a new song that was worth hearing, Dionisio cranked up the phonograph and put a record on, just loud enough to substitute for conversation.

After a while Pablo, their youngest brother, came in,

flushed from the feats and hazards of a twelve-year-old's existence. He greeted Jaime shyly, answered a few polite questions. (He was through school, and was only waiting to grow up and be a motorcycle rider.) But with Dionisio he was completely unreserved, treating him as a sort of lazy father worth more affection than respect. He seemed to think of Jaime as some vague uncle, toward whom these attitudes of respect and affection were reversed. He had little of either for old Guadalupe—merely the uneasy acceptance one might feel around a senile grandparent.

Dionisio sent him for some more pulque. Meanwhile his own wife, Sofia, appeared with the newly-walking twins, shepherded by the seven-year-old daughter who ran out back to play with Paz's giftling. Jaime endured the detailed questions of his sister-in-law concerning department store prices in Guadalajara which he didn't know, and motion pictures that he hadn't seen. Throughout this, Guadalupe submitted to the torment of his twin grandsons, who had tied his feet with a cord and were going through the motions of building a fire under him.

Now Pablo returned with the pulque, in company with his niece, Dionisio's fifteen-year-old daughter. She had a gringo child she was nursemaiding, and when it began to squall uncertainly at the noise and confusion she gave it some pulque. It quickly fell into a contented sleep. Then she put on a recording of the Zacatecas March and called her younger sister in to dance with her. Presently there was the sound of ad-

ditional chickens being slaughtered in the yard. Above
all this, Pablo conducted a cross-examination of the
twins:

"*Quién á esta casa da luz?*" Who gives light to this
house?

"*Jesus!*" They screamed the rhyme in unison.

"*Quién la llena de alergria?*" Who fills it with happi-
ness?

"*Maria!*"

"*Y quién la cuida con la fe?*" And who guards it with
faith?

"*José!*"

Barnaby Kidd is right, Jaime thought. I've lived
around Americans too long. And even as he pronounced the word to himself, *Americanos,* he heard the
quotes around it. Imagine a people arrogant enough to
appropriate the name of an entire continent for their
exclusive use. And worse, imagine a world being awed
enough to accept it.

But by mid-afternoon, animated with pulque and
ravenous from the smells that seeped from the kitchen,
he was a reborn man when Paz, Sofia, and his mother
came in like an Aztec processional, bearing steaming
bowls of chicken swimming in the chocolate-dark red
fiery sauce that hadn't changed within the last millen-
nium. He could even say grace, when his mother
timidly asked him, and looking at the table spread before him, for the moment mean it.

As they all fell to, Dionisio picked up a fierce green
jalapeno and grinned at Jaime. Jaime also took a pepper

from the jar, and they matched each other in devouring them, another, then three more, feeling the delicious searing in the palates.

"*Cosquillas* tomorrow," Dionisio laughed. "What is hot on entrance will be hot on exit."

"*Sí, mano*," Jaime said, constricted with affection and the exquisite afterburn.

Lifting a dripping chicken breast from the common bowls with a tortilla, Jaime thought, well, we can cook. We can do one thing better than the whole world. And he was content enough to pity the poor *Americanos*, who could only warm their stomachs with a money belt.

IT ALWAYS
COMES OUT
DIXIE

When Joel turned fourteen, there was still a Depression throughout the land. He was made awkwardly aware of it by the newsreels and the radio's hushed urgencies, or his father's sudden economies and his mother's charity drives. But mostly it bypassed him. Berkeley, California, was a university community owning a police force equipped with several quaint and quasi-legal statutes defining vagrancy, and Joel's father owned the second best department store in town. Joel had no intention of succeeding to it, however, much as it would hurt the old man when the time came. By then he figured to be, not necessarily the most exciting trumpet man in jazz, but certainly one of them.

Toward that end he had acquired a second-hand King cornet. His folks regarded it as one more passing phase, along with the abandoned crystal set and the chem lab in the basement. But to their uneasy surprise, Joel quit the track team and reinvested the time (and wind) in tunneling through an instruction book. At the end of a year he had come out through its back cover, the exercises no longer offering much challenge. Those first wobbly arpeggios were crisp and clean now, the high notes brilliant and the below-the-staff tones fat and rounded. When he entered Berkeley High, he immediately joined the dance band.

It was supervised by Miss Morton, the *a capella* instructress (now known, inevitably, as Jelly Roll Morton). Joel had been beaten out for lead trumpet in auditions by a senior with a nice schmaltz tone, but he was more than happy to settle for the second spot, the hot man. However, rehearsal periods were spent in the woodshedding of what Miss Morton thought were "nice songs" for football rallies, and "Empty Saddles in the Old Corral" or "Moon Over Miami" offered dim opportunities for a man to take a ride chorus. Those seriously concerned with jazz stayed after school to form their own group.

It drew random visitors to the music annex, and after awhile Joel began noticing a steady spectator. He was a colored kid, a freshman like himself, who seemed especially interested in Joel's playing. His name was Elroy Sims. They got in the habit of having a smoke together, after the janitor would lock up, in the malt

shack across the street. Elroy was the first Negro that
Joel had had a chance to really talk to, and after their
shyness had worn off they'd go into music at great
length before splitting up. (They lived at different
ends of town.) Elroy's feeling for jazz was only an
onlooker's; he didn't have the money for a horn of any
kind. But he knew a lot of sidemen—not personally,
but their styles and ideas. There were some local
colored musicians he thought Joel ought to try and
catch. They agreed to meet the following Saturday at
Sweet's Ballroom in Oakland, where the East Bay Esquires were playing a race night gig. Joel had no
trouble getting in. (They were prepared to claim he
was an octoroon, but no one asked.)

Up till then, Joel had naturally assumed that
colored trumpets were overpraised exceptions, like
colored poets. But history became myth the moment
he heard the Esquires lean into their opening theme.
He didn't know where all that sound could come from
with just four brass, five reeds, four rhythm. And tow-
ering above the whole vast impact was a young, tall,
coal black man with a golden trumpet, a handful of
polished plumbing that made Joel's scalp lift. *Don't
he send you, man?* Elroy kept shouting, his face shin-
ing with sweat and abundance, like all the faces
crammed below the bandstand, and Joel could only
wish he *were* an octoroon.

He rode back with Elroy on the Grove Street owl
car in a subdued mood. The trumpet man, he learned,
was a San Franciscan named Monroe Bluett—practi-

cally a next-door neighbor of one of Elroy's cousins. Joel took down the address, and Monday morning when his mother came to wake him, he was already dressed.

There was an autumnal bite to the air as he left, supposedly for school. Carrying his cornet case, Joel got off the streetcar at Shattuck Square and boarded an orange Key System train that rumbled past boarded-up store fronts and deserted pee-wee golf courses, through the wastes of West Oakland till, hurtling along the narrow trestle than ran invisibly and thrillingly above open water, it slid into the Oakland Mole.

Stepping down into the smells and bustle of the gloomy yellow shed, he let the surge of passengers scoop him up the gangway to the deck of a squat orange ferry boat. Leaning out past life boats with their rusted davits, he watched the fat limed pilings, gull-roosted in the widening light. Then the murky water below began to lather and the orange peels dance like vegetables in a mulligan, and he braced himself against the white deep blast of the whistle. He laughed, seeing the gulls launched from their stupor, flapping and screaming in suspicion that the ferry, having fattened them for so long, was now about to turn on them. But the old boat warped from the shuddering, creosoted piles, hooting a path before it; and the gulls returned down airy spillways; grey wings and white breasts flashing as they swooped and pivoted in retrieve of fragments tossed from lunch bags, or like great sea moths haunted lower portholes for the steward's slops.

He dodged past the jumbled baggage carts to the forward rope, then in a random frenzy of excitement hurried topside to rub a keyhole in the fogged glass and follow the swinging buoys in the shoals. Now he could see the bulk and sprawl of San Francisco, pushing out of the bay and its own pale vapors. On the blurry edge of assemblage, the City arrived down its hills in banked white terraces to the waterfront. Back out on deck, Joel waited while the white-butted Frisco wharfscape, mellowed from the sea's long use, heaved into place. A deckhand dropped the restraining rope and then they were stampeding down the asphalt ramp into the Ferry Building where time stared four directions from its tower, and streetcars shuttled down the clanging hub to meet them.

Just in case he was a little early, Joel treated himself to a hamburger: a real one (not some thick, bland wedge of ground round), with all the mixed smells of the griddle and the bun greasily hot. He had seconds on a cup of coffee with it, thought about thirds, then surrendered his dime to the bored counterman. A newspaper peddler with a World War overseas cap gave him directions, and Joel hopped a Geary streetcar out to the Fillmore district.

Here there was a great hushed lack hanging over the streets. Not of people, because men were out in large numbers—all colored, and lounging against the walls in twos or threes or just walking around in their springy way. A lot of them were pretty well dressed. They all seemed to be waiting for something. Now and then a younger colored woman would switch by, and if a man knew her he might fake a grab for her elbow, or maybe walk partway to the corner while they kidded. There seemed to be a lot of kidding going on. While he was standing there a very dark Negro, darker than Monroe Bluett, even, passed two men underneath the awning of a Texas Bar-B-Q. One of them nudged the other and said, "Give him a quarter, man, he's bluer than you." Joel grinned uncertainly. They grinned back, and he produced the address hoarded in his wallet.

It turned out to be the next block over on Buchanan Street, a yellow frame house with a divided lawn. Joel rang the bell in nervous excitement. After awhile a bulky Negro lady opened the door and leaned against it. She glanced down at his cornet case and half-closed her eyes.

"I hope you ain't selling nothing, sonny," she said, "cause I can't afford it and I'm in no mood whatsoever for disputing."

"Oh no, it isn't that," Joel said quickly. "I just wanted to see Mr. Monroe Bluett—if he's in?"

"Well now, that puts a different complexion on the matter. Step this way and we'll see is he fixed for comp'ny."

Joel followed the woman down a worn-carpeted hall to a rear room. Slapping the door with a meaty palm, she called, "Mister *Mun*-row Bluett in there! Young man here to ask you for your autograph!"

She laughed soundlessly at Joel's embarrassment,

rattling the door knob till they heard muttering inside
and a shift of bedsprings.

Monroe poked his head out. "What's all this you
putting down, old lady?" Then he blinked at Joel, not
fully awake yet.

Joel couldn't ask him in front of the landlady, or
whoever she was. "Can I talk to you in private?" he
blurted.

Monroe stepped back in surprise, and when he was
inside Joel set his cornet down. Keeping his eyes fixed
on it he said, "I, uh, heard you at Sweet's last Saturday
and, uh, I'm a trumpet man myself. That is, I play
some, and I thought maybe . . ." He swallowed and
finally got it out. "Could you teach me to play *colored*,
Mr. Bluett?"

He heard a grunt, looked up to see Monroe's face
crack open in a smile. "I can see what kind of day *this*
gonna be already," he sighed. "Sit tight, till I can
think a little."

He got a robe out of the closet and went into the
next room, where Joel heard a shower being run. While
he waited, Joel examined the room enviously, letting
his hands graze objects here and there: a cup mute
lying on the bureau, a white bow tie, a small electric
phonograph beside a stack of records. He'd have to
write the titles of those records down.

When Monroe came back, he had his snazzy red silk
robe on over his pyjamas and his hair was slicked in
place. His eyes still had that liquid, absent look,
though, only halfway up from sleep. He stood as if

listening, not quite as tall as Joel remembered him, but as black. Then with a loose flowing movement he picked up the clock beside the bed, shook it and turned to Joel.

"Oh, my. Ten-thirty?" he said reproachfully. "Don't you know a musician got to get his rest, man?"

Joel felt himself redden. "Gee, I didn't realize . . . Should I come back later on? That is, if it isn't . . ."

"No, now I'm up I guess it don't signify." He ran his eyes over Joel thoughtfully. "Now about your problem. You already know your horn, so all you asking more'r less is just some coaching how to riff. That summarize the situation?" he said, smiling.

"If you could spare the time, I'd sure be grateful."

"How much you figure I ought to charge you?"

"Whatever you think, Mr. Bluett," he said apprehensively, hoping his allowance would cover it.

"Let's do like this, um . . . what's your name?"

Joel told him.

"You got a dollar on you, Joel?"

"Oh, sure!" He reached for his wallet but Monroe waved it off.

"No, let's do like this. You go and take that dollar to the corner store and bring me back a pint of gin. The man'll know what kind, you tell him who it's for. Solid?"

"Solid!" Joel said happily.

He ran all the way, and when he got back the bed was made and Monroe was glancing through last week's *Downbeat*. He set it aside and took the pint from Joel, going into the bathroom and returning with a glass. Filling it about a third full, he drank the gin off in slow deliberate sips, sighed and set the bottle on the bed-table. Then he sprawled back with a pillow propped behind him and closed his eyes.

"All right, poppa Joel," he said dreamily, "play me something on that horn of yours so's I can tell how much I got to work with."

Joel snapped his case open with a feeling of eager-ness and misgiving. "It's just an old cornet," he stalled.

"Lots of fine men came up on cornets," Monroe mur-mured politely.

"I suppose." Wetting his lips, Joel blew a few show-off runs to warm up on, then said, " 'Honeysuckle Rose' in G okay? I mean *my* G."

"It's your dollar."

He filled his lungs, beat off an up-tempo bar with his foot and began. It was his favorite tune for jamming, and the key in which he knew his way around best. He stayed fairly close to the melody on the first chorus, getting the feel of the chord progressions, and on the second thirty-two bars he broke as free from it as he could, using the first valve for that nice flatted third whenever he could work it in. It was really a medley of his best phrases, echoing starkly in an anonymous room in a colored neighborhood, for the benefit of a man who, if not the greatest trumpet player in the world, would do till Joel heard better.

Finishing, he set the cornet down and watched Mon-roe's face, eyes still closed though he had been listening attentively. Now he sat up and swung his feet to the floor.

"I don't know, man. What do you think?" he said.

"I guess all it is is mostly Dixieland," Joel said hopelessly. "I can't understand; I don't particularly like to listen to it. But whatever I try, it always seems to come out dixie."

Monroe nodded. "Some good white boys around," he said, "technicians, mostly. But dixie don't do too much for me, either."

"Do I have any kind of chance at all?"

"Why surely, man. You're young. You just keep fighting all those evil influences, thass all."

Faintly encouraged, Joel saw him drag a trumpet case from underneath the bed and open it, exposing a sparkling gold Selmer nestling in its velvet. He ran his fingers over the valves, blew part of a little broken scale in a way that made Joel's heart skip.

"Now here's the way I personally would treat that tune, myself."

He raised the trumpet to his lips, tapped his foot until he found the groove that suited him, then started playing.

Instantly Joel's universe was filled with sound, a hoarse organic frenzy of it. The configurations were erected by a brutely flat tone, almost without vibrato, themes collapsing into one another while the melodic line ran through them like a sly thief. The echo of the last charged note hung on the air as Monroe finished and blew out the spit valve automatically.

"Oh, *yes*," Joel breathed, "gee, that was . . ."

Monroe smiled in appreciation. "It lays nice, that tune. Got some pretty changes."

"What was that thing you did—back there around the middle of the bridge?"

Monroe frowned, trying to remember. "Like this?" He picked up the horn and blew a two-bar cascade. It was entirely different, even better than before. Joel had him play it several times until he'd memorized it.

"Why it's just a plain D 7th with an added ninth," he said in surprise. An ordinary chord run up and down, but that lagged and crooked phrasing making something special out of it.

"Is *that* what it is?" Monroe said, impressed. "You see, I can't teach you music. All you need to learn is listening."

Refilling the toothbrush glass with gin, he settled back. Joel sat tensely on the edge of the bed. And now a tentative, caressing tone seeped from the trumpet's bell, dropped a husky octave and a blues began, whispering gutturally of aches and absences. The slim, groping fingers found the mood, the slightly puffed cheeks filled it full of langour, and in a key called F there were tender explorations of this word that small boys chalk on fences. Love went begging, some other footsteps sounded down the hall, and somewhere (the golden Selmer rumored) last month's moon filtered in on an empty pillow . . .

Monroe would pause, in the middle of a phrase sometimes, to take a drink and smile over at Joel; not quite seeing him, still back there. When the gin was halfway down the label, the door abruptly opened. A colored girl about Monroe's age sauntered in.

She smiled in apology. "I knocked, but I guess you didn't hear through all that ruckus. You just keep on, don't pay me no mind."

She walked over to the bed and Joel hastily made room for her. As she seated herself between them, Monroe slapped her on the fanny.

"Ruckus!" he said, "You can always plug your ears up."

"Why Monroe, you know how your playing affects me," she said, making her eyes large and misunderstood. "It drug me in right off the street, just like some old pied piper." She turned expectantly to Joel.

"Joel, this here's Crystal Bell Baker," Monroe explained.

"Very pleased to know you, Joel."

She extended her hand and he shook it, mumbling something in acknowledgment. He was irritated at the interruption, this overly familiar girl barging in on the understanding they were having. Now it was spoiled, naturally, with Monroe clowning around on his trumpet, ripping off high notes to impress her while she twiddled her fingers in his hair.

Then gradually, Joel found his irritation being drawn into a new dimension. The girl's thigh, as she squirmed in appreciation of Monroe's acrobatics, kept rubbing lightly against his leg. There was a plump firm feel to it beneath her skirt, and the intensity of his imagina-

tion made him think how it might look in just the night
light from the hall. He supposed he shouldn't think of
colored girls that way; still, he kept his leg rigidly in
place. From the side of his eye he watched her breasts,
tight in a faded cotton print. Creamy tan, they'd be,
and between, soft-shadowed . . . Joel looked up to see
her watching him with a faint smile. He flushed, and
her smile widened. Then Monroe laid his horn back
in the case, stood up and stretched. The girl moved
over slightly.

"Care for a little bit of sauce, baby?" Monroe sloshed
more gin into the glass and handed it to her.

She hesitated. "Well, I expect it wouldn't hurt to
cut the dampness." Sipping delicately, she lifted her
eyebrows in surprise. "Oooh, this is *smooth*. Must be
that dollar stuff."

"Surely is. Joel laid it on me for a music lesson."

"My gracious. Wish *I* could earn my dollars that
soft."

"Why sugar, don't you?"

"Be careful. I won't take that kind of language lying
down."

Then they both laughed for some reason, and the
girl turned to Joel.

"Monroe teach you a dollar's worth yet?"

"Oh sure," he said, "I only wish I could come over
every day."

"He learns quick," Monroe said. "Don't play too bad
at all right now."

Joel felt a rush of warmth, and the girl smiled differently than before.

"Well now, if Monroe say a thing like that it *got* to be true. Cause he just about the stingiest man for compliments I ever seen."

She probably was exaggerating, but it felt good just the same.

"Why don't you hit Crystal Bell with a couple choruses of something, Joel?" Monroe said suddenly.

"Now I'd just like that fine." She seemed to mean it.

Recklessly, Joel picked his cornet up from beside the bed and walked to the center of the room.

"What'll it be?" he asked Monroe.

Monroe considered the possibilities. "I tell you, man . . . do you know 'Honeysuckle Rose'? In a nice bright key, like maybe G?"

Grinning, Joel said, "Here it is."

And it was. He threw everything into it, eyes squeezed tight like Bunny Berigan (only imagining himself a sort of darker Berigan now, the Negroid inflections grafted on) as he booted it out, opening his eyes from time to time to see Monroe and Crystal Bell smiling tenderly, the way you watch a baby learn to walk. And he knew then, with the conviction of his entire life to date, that you *could* learn to think colored and by God some day it would come out.

He took three choruses, and on the last one, as a final garnish, he used that pretty D 7th lick of Monroe's in the bridge.

"My, oh my!" Crystal Bell said when he took the

horn off his lips, "that was just plain out of this world!"
She turned to Monroe. "And you know something? In
that middle part this last time round, there was one
place where he almost sounded just like you."

"He'll be all right," Monroe said quietly. "He got a
future." He held the glass of gin aloft to Joel and took
a thoughtful swallow.

"I'll drink to that, too," Crystal Bell said, taking the
glass from him. She lowered it an inch, then with an
odd challenging smile said: "Joel?"

Without hesitation he accepted the glass and finished
off the gin.

He felt it almost immediately, and through its spreading warmth he knew this was all he'd ever want from
life, this little and this much: to be the ride man in a
San Francisco jump band, waking at noon in his own
apartment with a whole night's choruses ahead of him,
and at the end of it a girl of his own, a product of his
horn. The way Monroe had it, who had everything
and who probably wasn't over twenty, just five short
years away . . .

But it never quite worked out that way. Before three
of those years had passed Madrid surrendered to a
strutting fat man; Finland was getting ready to sur-
render to her lumpish neighbor; Lou Gehrig surrendered from baseball, and Sigmund Freud, Zane Grey,
and Douglas Fairbanks surrendered from an overdose
of life. A year of surrenders, and Joel had long since
made his own. The cornet was in the basement, along

with the crystal set and the racks of crusted test tubes. Nothing much had ever happened with the horn, after that one gigantic Monday. All he could ever push out of it was dixie, although he never particularly cared for dixie. Occasionally, he'd wonder what happened to Monroe after the East Bay Esquires broke up.

He finally had that girl of his own, though, a nice white girl with nice white thighs. One nippy morning he drove her over the Bay Bridge to the Golden Gate International Exposition on Yerba Buena island. The bay below was clear, as far as you could see. The ferry boats were gone, along with most of their gulls, both being frills in an age of speed and seriousness. The Exposition was interesting and no doubt educational. After they'd been wandering through the exhibits for a couple of hours they passed the Danish Pavilion. Some workmen were on a scaffolding, painting a wall white. There was something gnawingly familiar about one of them, a tall, clowning Negro who slapped his paint on with a comic sweep. It was especially comical because he was so black against that vast white background.

A little knot of people had gathered to watch him, and finally one of them applauded. The Negro turned and doffed his stained cap to the crowd below. He didn't recognize Joel. But then of course he couldn't from that distance anyway.

"Getting tired?" he asked the girl. "Let's head back."

"But honey, don't you want to stay for the Benny Goodman concert?"

"Not particularly."

She was a redhead with a delayed way of frowning when she was confused. "But I thought you used to be a musician."

"That was a long time ago," Joel said.

She didn't get much conversation from him on the drive back. They made good time. The new convertible was a high school graduation present from his father. He'd be driving it to southern California this fall, where he was registering for a business administration course at U.S.C. His father's department store was still the second best in Berkeley.

THE VIGIL

When Tomás de Aquino Cuevas woke it was all at once. Apolinar was watching him from the foot of the rope bed with his serious eyes. Tomás threw back the serape that served both as bedcover and cloak against the pernicious night air, swung his feet to the brick floor and scratched his pantleg.

Apolinar scratched himself in imitation.

Tomás smiled. "How is the sickness, little one? Less bad?"

By way of answer, Apolinar coughed experimentally. But instead of clearing his chest it set off a racking series of coughs, the effort contorting his wrinkled face.

It had been that way all night, till Tomás fell asleep. He didn't know if Apolinar had slept at all.

Stroking the creature's back till the cough subsided, Tomás stooped over the brazier and fanned last night's embers into life. He sunk a bowl of water in the rosy charcoals, threw in a handful of coffee and when it was bubbling sluggishly he dipped it, half and half, into the jar of cow's milk. Calling Apolinar to the table, he set his mug before him and they sat over their café con leche like any pair of bachelors the wide world over.

It was a large room, more than ample for their needs, with high adobe walls for the sake of coolness and straw petates on the floor for appearance. There were two other families up front, and a community well out back with moon-flowers straggling down the waterline, which the widow Señora Podesta used to pick, banking them in limp white clusters around the room. She'd liked Apolinar, but the new Señora who came after didn't, very much.

When they were finished, Tomás wiped Apolinar's chest where he had dribbled and dressed him in the bright blue jacket like a sailor's, with bright brass buttons and the cap to match. It had been washed again the night before to remove the blood flecks. It still hung loosely on his wasted frame, though it had long shrunk. Then Tomás readied himself, strapping on the organ box he had inherited from his father.

The new Señora Gómez was sweeping down her doorsill angrily, as if the dirt had been a nocturnal gift.

She carried only one of two expressions, either anger or bitter contentment.

"Buenos días," Tomás said.

She looked up with her second expression and Apolinar skittered past her, eyeing the broom cautiously.

"There will have been no visitors for me?" Tomás asked with an air of concern. He wasn't expecting company, but he felt the possibility contributed to one's standing.

Señora Gómez turned, calling inside to her sister, a puckered twin who spent her mornings at the window watching for calamity.

"That there have been no seekers for the fool who keeps the monkey—the one smelly as the other and of which quién sabe is the master?"

The sister barked in appreciation as Tomás hurried Apolinar away from such incivility.

Going up the fitted slab stone sidewalk where grass stood between like bristles on a pig, he reflected that the world's words for the vulnerable were harsh. That he was lacking in alertness, he had known since childhood. School had been a confusion of impossible demands, with things no sooner memorized but that they changed, and he had early been excused from further struggle. He thought slowly, his ideas were few, but he was no fool. Señora Gómez was the fool, if she thought he believed that her husband was picking oranges in Texas and was ever coming back, to her with her tongue like the blister of a green pepper.

He paused and looked down at Apolinar. "What that

one needs for her redemption is a man. True, Chiquito?"

Apolinar hugged his tail around Tomás' ankle, chattering weakly.

"Ah well, it is nothing to us," he said. "We do not bring a candle to that funeral."

They continued through the wheel-cut streets, the one going slowly for the other's sake, the sun high over them and smouldering. Every little while Tomás would stop to grind a tune, less from the hope of attracting centavos in so poor a section than to let Apolinar rest. As he cranked, there would be lapses where the organ box made nothing, or at best, noise, till it caught again—often in a different key. And after all this time Tomás still winced in embarrassment, because it took only ears, not brains, to tell bad music, and he at least had ears.

He'd always hoped to be a real musician. Marriage had focused this ambition, and when he learned he was to be a father he took the hoard of pesos (the secret thumbworn pesos that the bank gave new ones for when he would ask), and bought a guitar. With it, he could raise his station in life and become a mariachi, a street singer. But his wife had died in bringing their dead son to birth, despite his pledge to Saint Ignacio of a silver key ring and a blameless life. And with their passing, all his luck—of finding a woman who could have it in her heart to value and respect him, who could raise a son to fill his years with dignity—passed also.

The guitar lay untouched and meaningless throughout the pair of lonely years that followed, till one day a traveling circus came to town. They had with them this beast who looked like some odd child locked in a dark brown coat, ill fitting and in need of patching. Too sick to perform well, too confused by the laughter and the shower of "gifts," his grave eyes caught and held Tomás all the way around the ring. Tomás stayed for two performances, and on the final one he returned with the guitar. Since it was in better condition than the monkey, the keeper traded instantly. There was a moment of regret at the loss of a mariachi's life, but one could not have everything.

Taking the high cobbled climb off the Street of the Clocks, they came now through the frothing alleyways behind the market, where lottery ticket salesmen called to lucky truck gardeners—their early melons sold at premium and their women leading home a piglet on a leash—*Fifty thousand pesos Tuesday, Aiee fifty little thousand* and if the buying had been brisk, a copper veinte would be thrown Apolinar to watch him scramble for it underneath an oxcart crammed with corn husks, one avid eye upon the coin and one upon the lumbering spokes above him.

They worked their way past canvas-covered stands where figs and mangoes lay in plump piles, between papayas opened down the middle and peanuts in small avalanches, till they gained the vast aisled marketplace itself. Here there was a constant tide of noise and smells: of corn roasting over coals, fresh-ground

peppers green and purple, of hot new breads and little
cheeses and of bucket-sprinkled greens. Tomás struck
up a tune and Apolinar quickened enough to lope
ahead, excited as always by the vivid racks of cloth and
beads and mirrors.

Their friends called out: Diego of the footwear, who
had a half banana that he'd saved Apolinar from lunch,
pretending to measure him for huaraches while he
watched him gulp it down; Santiago the Goalkeep, who
sold onions on the days there were no *futbol* matches,
and who had whittled for Apolinar a bladed little
wheel that turned in the wind of one's breath like a
windmill or the screw of an airship. And at her puesto
where dried herbs hung like withered baby hands in
bunches, and spices tartly hung the air, Tía Chepa
beckoned them over. They waited respectfully while
she sifted a fist of salt into the pot that was bubbling
for her siesta meal.

"Ven aquí," she told Apolinar. "Come, give me the
hand." She extended her hand and Apolinar took a
playful nip at it. She slapped him lightly. "Heed the
manners. Again!"

Apolinar chattered fretfully at her, then cautiously
cocked his arm forward. She enveloped his paw in
her canny hand and shook it gravely.

"Eso que sí," she said, "much better."

Apolinar leaped and wheeled in an excitement of
delight, then suddenly fell to coughing, with great rasp-
ing gouts that flecked his lips. Tía Chepa cradled him
to her roughly.

"Sí, sí," she said, "pobrecito." She reached inside his jacket. "Let me feel the chest." Probing it, she looked up at Tomás and shook her head. "Less well than ever. Each day he diminishes."

"No, he is better," Tomás said anxiously. "Truly."

"He cannot last. But if there had been better food and care . . . ."

"*Food?* He eats," Tomás said indignantly, "he eats the same as I. And more," he was now embarrassed, "because there are little animals in addition which he catches."

Tía Chepa only nodded.

"He was never well from the beginning. It was those malditos of the circus who neglected him. The fault is not mine."

"Of course, hombre," she continued nodding sadly. "And even before them, who knows? Guilt never falls to earth. It is always passed along."

"He will be better tomorrow. You will see." He reached down for Apolinar. "Let us go."

"He cannot last," she repeated calmly.

It had the strength of a curse, and it frightened Tomás. For while no one ever said that Tía Chepa was a bruja, a witch woman, no one ever said she wasn't.

They dropped down the gullied streets, the one talking softly for the other's encouragement, the organ silent. And at the plaza, with its fountains playing at each corner and the branch-lopped ash trees all along, they paused to taste the coolness. Here was the heart and pivot of the town, where the rockets and the *vivas*

towered on the Sixteenth of September, with boys and
unbetrothed girls passing clock- and counter-clockwise
in the flowered evening and the rockets echoing on
through September to drive all danger from the corn
harvest.

While Apolinar slumped in the bench's shade, list-
lessly dismembering a cricket, Tomàs eased his eyes
on the church that lifted opposite, its pink stone spires
converging at the cross whose bulbs at night burned
like a promise of undying faith, except on nights when
the electricity went out. Below, in the shadow of the
great old wooden doors where saints and cherubs
leaned from the rich stone lintel, beggars and taco vendors mingled their chants. And somewhere beyond
those doors stood Saint Francis himself, who, if one
had sufficient eloquence and a gift sufficient for his
trouble, could make Tía Chepa's prophecy come false.
But for a foolish, empty-handed man to disturb an im-
portant saint about an old woman's forebodings seemed
both blasphemous and wasteful. Besides, Apolinar
would get well someday; or if not well, not worse.

Comforted by this thought, Tomás turned to watch
the posada corner. From the built-up plaza he could
see into the second floor dining room, where Yanqui
millionaires partook of their unfathomable dishes in
the unalloyed gold candlelight, while those who understood their unfathomable tongue stood by to turn their
wishes into fact. Their automobiles were drawn up in
front, sleek and flawless, fitting all of one piece and

costing surely hundreds and hundreds of pesos every
one.

Now a Yanqui couple came down the marble steps
of the posada, paused aimlessly in the siesta-emptied
streets. The man was dressed in a coat of lamb's wool,
green and handsome as the belly of a leaf, and his
woman as expensively, though not so thoroughly. They
had with them a little boy who skipped ahead, arms
flapping in the manner of a bird, as all three crossed
the street and mounted to the plaza.

Tomás nudged Apolinar and shouldered his organ
box. When they came abreast he rose and began grinding vigorously. Apolinar scrambled from beneath the
bench, chattered excitedly and threw himself into a
clumsy cartwheel. The little boy shrilled in delight,
jerking at his parents' sleeves to halt them. The rich
asthmatic tremolo of *Over the Waves* filled the air as
Tomás waited to see if they were music lovers.

The man invoked the name of God in English.

Tomás cranked even more energetically until the
woman motioned him to stop. He did, a little hurt,
and the woman by way of apology smiled and said
what he realized must be:

"Buenas tardes."

"Muy buenas tardes," Tomás replied, and then introduced himself, as was proper. "Tomás de Aquino
Cuevas, in order to serve you."

The man asked his woman something. When she
murmured hesitantly, he grinned. Tomás waited, hoping
she would return to Spanish for that at least offered

opportunities for guessing. They were all smiling foolishly now.

The woman fanned herself self-consciously. *"Estoy
caliente,"* she said. " I am in heat."

Tomás flinched. "Sí," he murmured politely, "it makes
very warm."

She turned in triumph to her husband, who nodded
tolerantly while she talked. Meanwhile Apolinar had
stood up, facing the little boy and returning his solemn
inspection. They were almost the same height and
dressed almost identically—the North American boy in
a sailor's jacket like Apolinar's, though clearly of real
wool with the buttons no doubt of real gold. Now the
boy giggled shyly and put his finger in his mouth.
Apolinar raised his thumb and sucked it, in a perfect
imitation. The three adults laughed in unison.

"How many years has yours?" Tomás asked.

"What?" the woman said. "Oh, how many years has
my son? Four years," she smiled. "How many years
has the monkey?"

"The monkey? Equally," he answered. "Four years."

All the pleasure was gone. To them, Apolinar was
just a mimic of a man child. Even so, their own was
scarcely an improvement. Four years old, and still a
baby. Why, any boy of San Miguel with bones like
that and with that height would be age six or seven,
already capable of family chores.

Evidently encouraged by his parent's laughter, the
little boy began jumping up and down, screaming de-
mentedly at Apolinar, who matched him jump for jump.

They were on their hands and knees now, scrambling on the grass—when Apolinar was suddenly seized. His body shook with a fit of coughing, the worst yet, spraying the other one with a delicate pink froth. Calling aloud, the father ran over, yanked the boy to his feet and shoved Apolinar away with his foot. He addressed his wife angrily while she made soothing gestures.

Tomás sensed, as Apolinar must have, that they had offended the foreigners. Petting him, telling him through his hands that it had no importance, he started to leave.

"Señor!" the woman called.

He turned. She was urging something of her husband. The man sighed, reached in his pocket and tossed a coin behind him. Even before it landed, Tomás saw it was a five-peso piece. Apolinar quickly dug it out of a crevice in the walk, surrendered it only after a thorough inspection. He'd never seen one before.

Tomás hefted it in his palm, studying the silver profile of Hidalgo. He had the feeling that his dignity might have been trespassed upon, but if so it was through lack of culture rather than by intent, and five pesos was a more than suitable apology. It could buy a kilo of pork butter to make rich broths, it could buy hen's eggs enough so that Apolinar could have one every day for two full weeks. It was an amulet against disaster.

But it wasn't, quite. For when Tomás whistled Apolinar to him, he didn't come. He tried, dragging himself forward like a caterpillar. But the effort exhausted him and he sat, hurt and puzzled as he gulped for air. Tomás picked him up, surprised at how light he was. Then he moved off, using the familiar changeless limits of the homeward route to convince himself that things were safe, unchanged.

See, Chico, the goat of Cipriano at the watering place? We shall have a slice of her cheese for breakfast, and when you are well you shall have a ride upon her back like a vaquero. And see, how past the cornmill roof the birds run with the wind? It should be rain tonight; it should be good sleep.

They crossed the Calle San Francisco, on the first Street of the Clocks, and at number 72 the door gaped like a sleeper's jaw upon a pullet raising dust in the siesta heat, her off leg roped to a sunken cartwheel. Apolinar stirred in his arms and whimpered uncertainly.

They crossed Mesones, and the second Street of the Clocks began. Now number 72 lay on the opposite side. A scarred cat guarded its sill from an inquisitive dog, spitting at him from a distance but not risking any of her seven lives.

They crossed Insurgentes, descending the third Street of the Clocks, and from the window of number 72 the sister of Señora Gómez coldly watched them pass inside.

Here in the room with the high adobe walls where the sun only came at morning, Apolinar was taken with a chill. Tomás rubbed his limbs, then built up the brazier. But it made no difference. He laid him in the rope bed, swaddled him warm with the serape and sat at his side.

Elsewhere, there would still be light in the streets and the world going by beneath it. But here there were only the glowing coals, casting one's least movements on the wall, huge and irrevocable, mirroring one's sins of omission. In the banked red light Apolinar's eyeballs shone hot white; his chest whistled for air. And now Tomás pitched forward, striking his chest in a spasm of despair.

"Hijo, hijo mío!"

Then, through his grief, he heard a feeble answering sound. He looked up. Apolinar had raised his fists and dropped them on his breast in imitation. The room seemed all of one glow, the walls rosy and translucent like the threshold of hell. Tomás ran to the door.

"Señora, Señora!"

The Señora Gómez loomed at the head of the hall.

"That you should send quickly for the *cura*, to bring the final sacraments for Apolinar Cuevas. Hurry, por favor!"

"For whom? For *whom*?" The Gómez's face worked with rage. "Are you loco, that you seek unction for a brute even dumber than yourself? Barbarian!"

"Fruitless sow!"

"Assassinator! Head of a goat!"

"You need a man!" Tomás called wildly, slamming the door.

He stood for a vacant moment, watching the shrouded form through the shadows. Lighting a pair of candles, he set them at the foot and head of the bed. Then he quickly blew them out. Lowering himself to his knees, he raised his face and cleared his throat self-consciously.

"Hear me, then, Saint Francis," he said. "You know what he needs. Something to lift the sickness from his chest. I do not trouble you for miracles. Perhaps it would only take some little blessing that could be given quickly. At least if not to cure him, to keep him from . . . to keep him."

He paused, knowing he must be brief yet complete. "In money I have five pesos only. But I have in addition," he said hurriedly, "an organ of the finest quality. It is made of rare woods and has a voice like a choir." He felt the blood come to his face. "Actually, it plays very badly," he said, "but it is of sound construction. You realize I would not ask this of you if he were any beast whichever. But if he were of my very seed, he could not be more mine. If this is wrong, forgive me."

He waited for some sign that he had been heard and could withdraw. There was only silence.

"I will deliver the organ to you tomorrow morning, then. Provided, of course, that you fulfill your end. And now, with your permission, adiós." He climbed heavily to his feet.

There was nothing more to be done. Pulling a chair over beside the bed, he lifted the organ to his lap and began cranking it slowly. The music spilled out softly, lower in pitch than at its normal speed, like a sluggish stream of honey. He let his thought sail out on it, as he waited.

Apolinar opened his eyes and listened, as if he too were waiting.

After awhile Señora Gómez began pounding on the door and calling to him, and he began grinding faster and faster, drowning out the sound as he felt his good right arm pumping the sweat to his face and hoped that it was for the last time, that tomorrow the organ would be gone and he could start looking for some other kind of trade to keep them.

ON JORDAN'S STORMY BANKS

*f*leeing Phillie southward, leaving Pennsylvania for the second time in his life, thought Jason, the native son observes the home turf with some passing poignancy. Well, hell, why not? The cradle of liberty's done relatively right by me, and I'm relatively human. If you prick me, do I not bleed?

You provincial bastard, Jason told himself, in a smiling mood again. But still, there it was: the maze and sprawl of Philadelphia, filling the windows of the train to bursting; the streets he'd never rumbled in, being better built for classroom jousts than rumbling; the old man's dental parlor, with a waiting room with magazines the old man and his wife were capable of reading. The twig thus bent, young Jason had flourished into the white hope of the family. Being spaced properly had helped. His older brother was still a stock boy at Wanamaker's, the yeasty dream of business school long soured. Born in more prosperous times, Jason was now free and twenty-one, with a B.A. from the U of Pennsy just strong enough to hook a graduate scholarship at the hallowed ivy league academy in New Jersey. The twins, Hector and Hecuba, had just turned nineteen.

Hector was on the unsalvageable edge of punkhood. Frittering his way through high school, keeping street-corner vigils for the living he was taught was owed him, he was a dossier in search of a case worker. And Hecuba—what's Hecuba to me, that I should weep for her? She'd met a minister from South Carolina this year, married and followed him back to his rural pastorate. Now she was in jail. Served her right for all the Damn-yankee, Communist-inspired, Jew-financed ideas she'd been duped into. That had to be the explanation, because he'd read it in the newspaper. Ever since her arraignment he'd become a faithful subscriber of the paper of the town that held the county farm where she was being worked. No one was really informed unless he read a newspaper daily.

Am I my sister's keeper? Turns out someone has to be, Jason thought, watching the industrial outskirts level off into uncharted wastes that drank the Friday afternoon sun and waited for the population explosion.

But while I'm keeping her, I have two other keepings to take care of. I have to keep from getting killed, and I have to keep from getting castrated, spiritually or otherwise. If I go under, I go intact.

The capital of the land of the free in a December dusk, the traveler observes, is brisk with traffic, and in the depot waiting room train-bound and -stranded folk, both white and colored, eye one another with absentminded speculation or indifference. With neither, Jason eyed the passing ladies, now that there was a white young lady in his life.

Chick named Linda Faye Lovett, it turned out. Could that be she, that brittle blonde headed Dixiewards to Daddy for the week end? Or that calorie-burdened brownette with the PanAm bag and giggles —was that Linda Ofay Lovett? The coincidence would be too monstrous. And by the way, it would do no harm to give up chickwatching during one's Southern sojourn—though I'll be mothered if I'll lower my eyes for every single bitch that passes. Easy, he told himself, taking a few deep breaths for relaxation. It's just delay that gets the hackles up.

When the train was finally called for Charlotte, North Carolina, Jason got himself a window seat, although with night now, there was little to see. He broke open his polysi text, aware that with midterms behind him (his last one had been this morning), finals would be coming up all too soon. He was getting by, he supposed, though of course not as well as he had at Penn —not entirely owing to the difference between graduate and undergraduate work, he sometimes felt uneasily. But he couldn't give his full attention to the print. Suppose someone stopped in the aisle and said, *Ain't that a purty deep book for you to be areadin, boy? Ain't you skeered hit'll give you uppity ideas?* Well, he could admit that any book was a deep book to an illiterate. And he could go on to admit that he was a boy, although the law would regard him as grown enough to electrocute if he killed anyone. Now *I'll* ask you a question, Jason told himself. You smart-assed spade, what would happen to your scholarship if you drew a stretch on the chain gang? Why, that would depend on the justice of the sentence. Crazy, dad. Then let me ask you another. What would happen to your grades if you missed a month or two of school?

Irritably, Jason turned back to the chapter opening, trying to get some sense from it the second go-round.

The train pulled into the Charlotte depot a little after two a.m. In the lonely hour, as the traveler first set foot on Southern soil, he was fairly inconspicuous. He needed all the anonymity he could get, because even if he tried to help it, the clothes he wore and the way he carried himself would be a luminous chip on the shoulder. And in point of fact, the cab driver Jason ordered to the bus station kept studying him in the mirror with an amused curiosity.

Alighting, Jason gave him a contemptuously large tip, drew a couple of deep breaths and walked briskly into the bus station. Then, thrown off stride in confusion and relief, he saw a colored man talking with

the ticket clerk. As he walked up to them, he discovered that they were both beyond belief. The nigger
(the only word for him) was recounting some family
happening in an almost unintelligible dialect, waving
the bus ticket he'd bought and bobbing his humble
frizzled locks as Massah Tom chuckled his fat white
guts in condescension. Jason glanced around the waiting room, then saw it for the first time outside a photograph: a drinking fountain labeled *White Only*. Seated
nearby were a farm couple with a small girl asleep
in her father's lap, and a middle-aged man in a linen
suit with the look of a country lawyer.

Eventually, Charlie Coon finished his story and did
a darky shuffle out the door, presumably to wait there
for his public transportation, unless there was a colored
waiting room next door. Jason bought his ticket, was
told that the bus wouldn't leave until 4:30. He sat
down, read for five minutes, breathing deeply, then
got up and took a fifteen-second drink of water at the
fountain. The three adults wore looks of mild surprise
as he returned to his seat. The ticket clerk seemed
less surprised than hurt.

The man in the linen suit sat foward expectantly,
already beginning to smile, as if about to interrogate a
watermelon thief.

"Looky here," he said, "cain't you read proper, a
grown-up boy of your age?"

Jason, who had done his growing up with some
Mexican kids, cupped his ear with an apologetic smile.
"*Como?*" he said, then: "*Chinga tu madre, puto.*"

They waited uncertainly, the stupid crackers, almost willing to swear that he had asked for his bus ticket in right enough American. But because he had returned to his textbook (also in right enough, though pretty turgid, American), the linen-suited man could only turn restlessly to the farm couple and murmur,

"Must be one of them Nigra diplomats from up at the U.N."

"Must be."

"Seems like we're turning the whole world over to them."

"Seems like. . . ."

The room gradually began filling, and occasionally Jason heard newcomers being briefed on his political status. Shortly before 4 A.M. he glimpsed a state trooper standing beside him. Then he felt a hand laid lightly on his shoulder. He looked up. The trooper's face was calm and tired.

"Better wait outside, boy. We won't have any trouble that way."

As Jason moved to comply, he said, "Trouble from me, officer?"

The trooper shrugged, following him out the door. "From you or to you, same difference."

"You mean the victim is the guilty party down here? That's a law they haven't gotten around to yet in my home state."

The trooper nodded indifferently, walking off. "This isn't your home state. Leastwise, not yet."

After a moment he heard a phlegmy chuckle in the

darkness, turned to make out the form of Jigaboo Jim, the raconteur, leaning against a pillar.

"Oh my, when you fixin to sue the po-lice?"

"What minstrel show did you get your ass kicked out of?" Jason said.

"Same one you're in. They been kickin it, all right. But they never going to kick it *clear* out, yours or mine, don't worry bout *that*. Wouldn't have nothin left to kick."

"I'm curious about one thing. How many pounds of crap a day does it take to feed a nigger?"

"You might could tell me."

"God damn you," Jason said in a furious whisper, "I'm not a nigger. I'm a human being."

"No you not, or you'd say it louder." The chuckle again. "The human bean's are all sittin down in-side."

Christ, what this trip is doing to me, he thought. Will I ever be able to have white friends again?

Along toward 4:30 his bus, which originated here, was thrown open for loading. Jason boarded it, took an inside seat in the exact geometric center. As other passengers came aboard, Jason noticed—puzzled at first, then thrilled to the point of wanting to whoop—that colored people never sat together. They would spread out over the bus and, by occupying the empty double seats, force white passengers to either sit with them or stand. A number did stand, and since it was a long and punishing ride through a December-dreary land-scape, their feet had plenty of time to hurt while his paisanos lounged at their ease and chatted across the

aisles. Jason, however, was joined by a white grand-
mother-type who sat looking grimly ahead the whole
trip. Since he restrained himself from attacking her,
he might have made a moderate out of her by the time
they arrived.

It was 8:30 when the Righteous Traveler descended
the bus to the more belligerent of the Carolinas, and
the R.T. was simply not about to breakfast at a cafe
catering to minstrelmen. But because it might have
been too early an hour for calling, he took a long walk
through a town in a state that was completing his education. The houses for the most part were neat and
faded, a generation behind the times and furnished
with appropriate inhabitants. But their faces, as he
forced himself to meet them squarely, seemed to re-
flect an angry bewilderment.

At an unlabeled public telephone Jason looked up
Judge Lovett's address, then stepped into the hotel
next to the bus station.

"A rather quaint little town you have here," he told
the desk clerk in a British accent. "Somewhat poverty-
stricken compared to the rest of the country, but I suppose your lack of industry keeps you stagnant. I may
stop over for a few days. What is the rate for your
rooms?"

The clerk, a balding brachycephalic with the complexion of a sunburnt baby's prat, shook his head.
"We don't have no rooms."

Jason laughed in goodnatured contempt. "You're a
bloody liar, my man."

The clerk turned purple from the novelty of it all, then stalked into an adjoining office. Jason hesitated, preparing to cut out. Maybe he had gone too far. But another man emerged to greet him with a wary smile.

"Are you connected with the U.N., by any chance?"

"I am a national of one of the republics that comprise the United Nations," Jason said.

"I reckoned that was the case. Well, I'm sorry, mister, but we're usually booked up pretty far in advance. There's a motel just outside town that most always has a vacancy, if you'd like me to call a taxi."

"That would be damned decent of you, old sport," said Jason, settling for the microscopic triumph before it turned stale.

With an eye for Jason's ease, the administrator of the crammed-to-capacity hotel selected a cab driven by someone of Jason's hue, who deposited him at Judge Lovett's home on Cherry Lane. It was a modest, white frame house ("gracious," the society page had called it), and Jason rang its bell, too keyed-up to breathe deeply or behave in any other organized way. After awhile the door was answered by the judge himself, older than his photo but still recognizable by the broad, untroubled forehead and the chivalrous nose dividing, like a watershed, calm eyes that never had the need to overflow. There had been no photos of the other members of the family.

"Yes?" A cordial, resonant voice before which only trouble-makers need quail.

Playing it by ear, determined that any consequences

were beyond consideration, like outrageous luxuries, Jason said,

"I'm afraid I need some advice, Judge."

The judge hesitated, then smiled quickly. "I was just about to fix myself a pot of coffee. Will you join me in a cup?"

"That's very kind."

Leading him back to the kitchen, the judge said, "Please have a seat. I b'lieve we can be more comfortable here, with less chance of interruption." The incomplete comparison, as endemic in Dixieland as on MadAve: Pukies taste crunchier, the kitchen is more comfortable—than what?

"I don't b'lieve I've seen you before," the judge said idly, measuring coffee at the immaculate sink. "Are you new to this locality?"

"Completely. I have a sister in agriculture here, whom I intend to visit. But I felt that visiting you had higher priority." Jason watched him put a flame under the coffee pot. "By the way, Judge, we aren't about to break the law, are we? Haven't Negroes been jailed for attempting to drink coffee with their superiors?"

The judge's smile hardened, but remained in place. "I'm afraid you're the victim of misinformation. We don't regard any race as superior or inferior here. We merely acknowledge that they're different. I realize other areas of the electorate refuse to acknowledge a difference, but South Carolina isn't wealthy enough to be unrealistic."

"Why not?"

"Because we got licked in a war. But you didn't come here for a debate. I b'lieve you said you needed my advice?"

"Yes, here's my situation," Jason told him. "I've just begun my Ph.D. in political science at Princeton. I think it's the road to a career with an unlimited future. In government, for instance, with all the new African nations . . . ." The judge was nodding noncommittally. "But that's several years away. I'm a scholarship student, and my family helps me out as much as it can, so I'm getting by financially. But meanwhile, my girl has gotten herself pregnant."

The judge smiled, shaking his head in commiseration.

Jason smiled back. "That was an ungallant way to put it. Subconsciously trying to weasel out of it, I suppose. Oh, I know she's played around plenty—she was a long way from a virgin when I met her. But I have no doubt that I'm the father."

He stood up and began pacing, as if to stretch his legs, but actually to keep the kitchen table between them. "She could quit school and work for awhile till the baby comes." he said thoughtfully. "That would take care of the hospital bills. We could squeeze by, I guess." He paused and looked at the judge. "Or, we could play it safe, get an abortion and wait for a planned family with a financial cushion for it."

The judge waited. "Is that your question to me?"

"That's it."

"Then I say forget the abortion. It's illegal, it's dangerous, it's expensive, and it'll leave scars on both of you."

"Thank you, Judge. I was hoping you'd see it that way. And underhanded as it was, I hope you'll understand why I delayed introducing myself. I didn't want your opinion to be colored by emotion." He smiled bashfully. "This is a hell of a time to tell you, but I'm Bill Basie."

The judge looked puzzled. "Should the name mean something to me?"

Now it was Jason's turn to be puzzled. "Didn't Linda Faye write you? I'm your future son-in-law."

Right between the motherloving eyes. It was a spectacle worth coming seven hundred miles to see.

"I don't b'lieve you," the judge said, punch-drunk. Then the sound of the words partially revived him. "How did you meet her?"

"New Jersey's a small state, Judge. Especially in college circles. One of her sorority sisters at New Brunswick—a colored girl I'd known—invited me to a dance, and there was Linda, looking perfectly *linda* —that means beautiful in Spanish, as you know—and," he shrugged, "it was love at first sight."

He was hoping the judge would ask him the name of his daughter's sorority at the New Jersey College for Women. But the judge, considerably older than he'd been when he'd answered the door, seemed bludgeoned into tentative acceptance.

"I can't b'lieve it," he said, and since this was irrele-

vant, he overruled himself. "How long—how far along
is she?"

"A little over two months, so it'll be a seven-month
baby. Happens every day, because the seventh month
is often—"

"It won't be any kind of baby."

Now Jason felt the full force of the judge's contempt.
It stunned him into impotence, until anger quickly
gave him back his strength. He assumed a shocked
expression.

"Why, Judge, abortion is as illegal as a sit-in. What
made you change your mind? Shouldn't we talk it
over with my future mother-in-law first?"

The judge bent with a wince, as if he'd gotten a
stomach cramp; then he straightened, rose from his
chair and walked out to the hall. Jason stepped after
him, heard him attempting to put through a long distance call. Since it was Saturday (and he hoped it
was beautiful weather in New Brunswick), with any
luck Judge Lovett's daughter would be away from her
sorority house. Christ, wouldn't it be perfect if she
were off on a shack job somewhere for the entire
week end?

Now he noticed, propped on a kitchen cupboard near
some letters, a tinted photograph of a mousy, chubby
ash blonde with dental braces, who, if she was Linda
Faye Lovett, was pretty unlikely to be off on any shack
job. He leafed quickly through the letters, found one
with her return address. Poor unlucky Linda, her language was as drab as her looks; it was taking time to

make new friends at college, the weather was simply horrid, and she missed them both so awful. . . . Smiling gently as he read the misspelled schoolgirl scrawl, he thought, Why, she's worse off than Hecuba, because *her* stretch in a life sentence. Jason sighed. The hell with it, he decided. I've got what I came for, the coffee break is over.

Then he sensed the presence of the judge behind him. He turned, flushing, and stuffed the letter back into the envelope.

"Just wondering why she hasn't had the courage to write you about us," he mumbled.

Ignoring the act and the remark, the judge reseated himself at the table and waited stiffly. Now Jason was hungrily aware of the aroma of coffee. He found cups and saucers in the cupboard, spoons at the drainboard, set the table and poured.

"Thank you," the judge said, sipping absently at his cup. He set it down hard, spilling half of it. "I'm warning you that you can consider yourself my house prisoner. If you attempt to leave before I talk to my daughter, I'll order your arrest. When I get hold of her, I'll see that she comes home immediately. There will be no excuse for marriage."

Jason finished his coffee deliberately, letting his reactions settle. Meanwhile, the judge remained fixed in place, as if posing for a slow-exposure camera study.

"I'm trying to understand your position, sir," Jason said honestly. "Don't you ever allow for exceptions? Try to look at it this way. In just a few short years I'll have a doctorate from an Ivy League university. It could eventually bring me an income five times yours." The judge nodded slightly, not contesting it. Encouraged, Jason said more deferentially, "I have a future better than that of any white man Linda could attract." He hesitated awkwardly. "Let's face it, she's no movie star. Neither am I, but men don't have to sell their looks for security. Women do. Along with an ability to conduct an intelligent conversation. I think Linda's lucky that I love her." When there was no response, he said, "Look, we won't be living down here. We'll be traveling in governmental circles; probably abroad. All this, of course, completely aside from the fact that you don't own her and she happens to be in love with me."

Caught up in the script he had created, banqueting in foreign embassies with a marble-skinned Galatea he had masterfully shaped from adolescent fat, malocclusion, and mangled syntax, he waited for the judge's begrudged acknowledgment of reason. After which, Jason could magnanimously consent to her abortion, promise to reconsider their engagement, then take off, stopping just long enough to pass the word to Hecuba. When it spread, it would get the sit-ins through their remaining days a little faster.

The judge turned to him. "I own her. Just as she owns me. And I'm a trifle too old to learn my responsibilities from an outsider, regardless of his blood. I don't say this lightly, but before I see her in miscegenation

I'll see her in her grave. And if I have to see her in hers, I'll see you in yours."

Abruptly, Galatea's face relapsed to unworked dough, her scrawny lips gaping in abhorrence as she cried ray-yip! ray-yip! in her father's twangy diphthongs.

Carefully pouring and sugaring another cup of coffee, Jason drank half of it before he sat back with a conciliatory smile.

"Well, at least we can agree that our first concern is Linda's well-being. I didn't mean to come down so hard on her deficiencies," he said, "but a parent can't always see them. I can love her in spite of her faults, just as you can. She can't read anything beyond the level of a movie magazine, her tastes are hopeless, she can't speak two consecutive sentences in English, but she can't be blamed for being ignorant. What was there in her background to give her any glimpse of civilized living? Oh, she'll straighten out eventually, of course," he chuckled indulgently. "Right now, she's a rebel. Kicking off family restraints, I guess. Strews her clothes all over the floor, goes for days without bothering to take a bath. Personally, I kind of like it. It gives her a nice, funky smell. But there's one thing I don't suppose you know about her," he said earnestly, "and it makes all her defects seem beside the point. She's just about unbeatable in bed."

The judge slumped forward, holding his face in his cupped hands. "Please don't speak to me for awhile."

It was a pleasure to oblige him. Jason wanted

nothing more than just to sit and watch those contorted shoulders.

But twenty minutes later the phone rang, and when Judge Lovett hurried to it and didn't return, Jason knew the jig was up. The jigaboo was up, to be precise. This was the part of the trip that he hadn't rehearsed, and now he wished he had. Well, it was a nice ride while it lasted. Too bad Linda Faye wasn't more popular Saturday mornings.

The judge came past him like a halfback sprinting for a garbage pass. Jason stuck his foot out too late. He knew he'd never make it halfway to the nearest ditch, but he didn't even get the chance to try. He'd just got the kitchen window up, got a leg over the sill, when he heard the judge shout *Halt!*

Jason froze, his back muscles bunching as they braced for the impact of both muzzles. Breaking and entering, he thought in despair, he'll say I came through the window. He started to fall, then opened his eyes in disbelief and steadied himself. Moving with the utmost caution, unable to control his trembling, he pulled his leg back inside, slowly closed the window and raised his hands high in the air.

"Shoot me in the back," he said, "you can't miss. You're a brave man, murder me."

"I nearly did," the judge said in awe. "I b'lieve I nearly did."

Keeping his hands in the air, Jason turned around. The judge lowered the pistol he was holding, set it on the table and folded into a chair. His head was sunk between his arms.

Jason dropped his hands. "That's not the way to kill a nigger," he said. "Not man to man. That brings you down to the nigger's level. You have to get a dozen other men to help you, and you have to get drunk first so you can have the guts, and even then, you have to all wear masks. Then you tie the nigger to a tree," Jason chanted, "you cut his nuts off, shoot him in the belly, and burn him while he's still conscious. *That's* the way to kill—"

But the judge was weeping openly now, a grown man grieving that he'd nearly taken life or been prevented, crying out in relief that his daughter was still unmongrelized, crying out anticipation of the nightmares for the next four years of Northern college life, for didn't *he* know the hidden hankering for black flesh, and wasn't she her father's daughter?

There was a scrap of toilet paper behind Judge Lovett's left ear lobe, evidently stuck there to staunch a shaving nick. His thinning hair, combed to cover his spreading baldness, wasn't too successful at the job. Jason resented having to see him as only a man of ordinary vulnerabilities.

The judge sat upright, his face drawn but under control again. "But why," he said incredulously, "*why?* What kind of monster are you?"

A jovial-looking woman in a flowered hat came in from the hall. "Excuse me, dear, I didn't know you had—" She hesitated uneasily in the doorway as her eyes rested on the pistol.

"Everything's perfectly all right," the judge said calmly. "There's nothing wrong at all, but please send for Hobie Yandle."

She exchanged a quick look with him, then shut the door. Jason could hear her start to dial.

The judge put the pistol in a nearby sideboard. "I'll ask you again. What was your purpose in perpetrating such a vicious practical joke?"

"It *was* a joke, wasn't it?" Jason glanced at his watch. "But you had just a measly half hour of it. How would you like it day in and day out for sixteen days, with fourteen more to go? That's the joke you played on my sister. I'll have to admit that yours was funnier."

"Who is your sister?"

Jason merely gave him an unamused smile.

The judge reddened. "I resent your insinuation. You are the only one answerable for your crimes. The law doesn't use kinfolk for retaliation."

"Doesn't it? I do."

"Don't worry, it's nothing that you can't be cured of," the judge said. "Now, you imply I gave your sister a thirty-day sentence. What did I think she was guilty of?"

"Delusions of grandeur."

The judge sat back. "Was she by any chance among the group of trespassers in the drug store incident?"

"Not until she'd finished her shopping at the cosmetics counter. She became a trespasser when she reached the soda fountain. When you decided that, I knew you had a remarkable sense of humor. Who's Hobie Yandle?"

"He's our chief of police," the judge said. "He'll give you the opportunity to have an extended visit with your sister."

"And then we start all over again?" Jason asked, surprised to discover that he still hadn't run out of adrenalin. "What kind of jokes do you think that will make me capable of when I get back to New Jersey? Or if I decide to come down here again?"

The judge got quickly to his feet, his face stiff with anger. "You're really asking for it, aren't you?"

"You see, we're finally down to the language of diplomacy: 'If you want a war, you can have one.' We're at war now, judge," Jason said unhappily, feeling that it was probably true and wondering how it had come about. "Let's not have any escalation. You had your chance to kill me. If you can't do it now, let me go. There's no stage we can stick at in between."

The front doorbell rang.

"You've committed a crime," the judge said stubbornly. "I'm not sure what to call it. Maybe not a grave one, but a crime, nevertheless. As an officer of the law, I cannot condone it. Nor can I as a man."

"Kill me *before* I give you grounds," Jason insisted quietly, "not *after*. That'll be too late for both of us."

The judge set his face grimly and started for the door to the dining room.

"Wait!"

When the judge paused, Jason said: "Then I'll do it for us." He had come around to the sideboard where the pistol lay. "We're condemned to a suicide pact of one kind or another, so why delay it?"

His eyes wavering, the judge smiled uncertainly. "Because I think you're too intelligent."

"Of course—*this* time," Jason agreed. "This time I'm just pretending. You hurt someone I love. I pretended to hurt someone you love. You *did* it. I only *pretended*." Now he allowed himself to fill with fury. "Why, you arrogant son of a bitch. Does that make you think I'm only capable of loving and hating in pretense? Do you still seriously think you people have a monopoly on emotions? If you can't give me life imprisonment right now, in an escape-proof jail, then we're in trouble. Take another look at me. I'm not a South Carolina Bible student. What do you think a year on a rock pile would do to me? You just don't *carry* that much insurance."

As the judge stared at him in baffled injury, the door behind him opened and a cop leaned half his bulk inside, his right hand resting lightly on his holster.

"Be of any assistance to you, Judge?"

"What? Oh, thank you kindly, Hobie," he said absently, "just give us another minute." When the door closed, he leaned against it for a weary moment and shut his eyes. Then he stood erect, facing Jason with an air of resignation. But what he was resigned to, Jason couldn't tell.

"Even if I could forget that I'm an officer of the

law," he said, "I'm still a man." He waited in mild expectancy.

"So am I," Jason told him. "But you've been one longer than I have. Three centuries longer, so you don't have to prove it. I do."

The judge nodded expressionlessly, turned and strode into the dining room. "Follow me."

And walking lightheadedly the distance to the front door, Jason wondered whether some day, at an hour too late for clairvoyance, it would turn out to be the distance of the corridor from the last cell to the little green door in Columbia, South Carolina.

The police chief, who'd been standing at the parlor entrance chatting with Mrs. Lovett, turned as they came through. The judge held the front door aside for them, and all three stepped out onto the porch. A prowl car with another cop was waiting at the curb.

The judge glanced at Jason. "You came through Charlotte?"

Jason nodded.

"See this man aboard the first bus to Charlotte, Hobie."

The police chief began grinning.

"And Hobie," the judge said sharply, "nothing else. Just see him aboard."

"You're the doctor, Judge," the chief said with a trace of disappointment.

And riding toward town in style with a pair of liveried escorts, Jason decided it was just as well he hadn't got to see his sister. It would only weaken her, make her want out that much more. And he wanted her strong enough to prevail over those of her color who were somewhat more extreme. The boys who really played dirty.

HONOR BRIGHT

*E*lbows propped on his knees, large hands cradling a clay cup, Luke Regan listened vacantly to church bells dissolving on the rippled air. He woke by degrees, from the center out. The warmth on his palms merged with the sun on the glazed brick floor, the weave of his robe with the mat's. His eyes converged on the white-washed wall, his head dipped to the cup. Energy flowed into him like strong dark coffee. Metabolism purred. He was alive, his juices singing sweetly in their channels.

"Ofelia!"

"Speak, señor." The maid appeared at the kitchen archway.

Luke pointed at the table.

"Breakfast, then?" she asked.

"You washed your hair," he said in his most peccable, Missouri-flavored Spanish.

Ofelia straightened her red bow complacently. "Would you wish to (something) with papaya for the (something else) and of eggs how many in what style?"

"You smell exciting. Let us have orange juice, and an end of papayas."

She tossed her head. "I smell like I smell. We have no oranges, they (something) very dear and ugly. And besides they lacked in juice." In other words, why should orange-vendors share the kitchen budget when her uncle was the owner of a small papaya grove.

"All right," he said. "Let us get married."

"The eggs, señor."

"Three, beaten. With sausage and many rolls."

She disappeared with a fetching flounce, returned with a wedge of papaya. Toothsome little beast, Luke thought experimentally, and grinned at finding that he was Gauguin this morning. But even after two full weeks in Mexico, he couldn't take his surroundings seriously. Those mangoes in the low-fired bowl—beautifully handled free forms, with sliding highlights on their slipped ellipses and in all the interior-decorator tones of chartreuse. Surely they were no more edible than stage props. Or his daily centerpiece of orchids, crammed in a tumbler like a child's bouquet, their petals flecked with dew and dishwater. Or especially this Indian virgin named for Hamlet's sweetheart, catering to his wants (to the extent that he could keep them conventional and understood) for the sum of ten far-fetched dollars a month. Too bad you couldn't smuggle all of it across the border.

Drenching the papaya in lime juice, Luke tried a spoonful. Its sour-acid, predigested taste hadn't changed. Food only fit for young birds.

But he'd still sneak the climate back with him. The sun that human hearts had fattened for so many centuries, and that brought the landscape to its slow flat temper. The dust, like none he'd ever seen, like a separate pigment as it spread that same sun over Lake Chapala. And the colors of Zopilotl, harsh and clashing to the point of melodrama. Yet even in its name, the Aztec word for buzzard, this was a melodramatic village. Some of these things, he hoped, were in the oil he'd completed yesterday. It was waiting on its easel, below the skylight, for his final judgment.

There was a knock at the door, the hesitant light knuckles of a Mexican. After awhile Ofelia came through, patting her hands dry on her skirt. The caller was a child, in a double-wrapped rebozo that fell all the way to her feet. From magic depths she breathlessly produced an egg.

"Good day my mother says if you don't want to buy an egg?"

Ofelia fiercely protected her *patrón* who, being vastly wealthy, was no fool. Was it fresh, this egg? Clearly, the hen had just now put it, feel its warmth. How much, then, for the puny thing? Fifty-five centavos.

Are you mad, that I don't know those hens it came from? *Pues*, fifty centavos then. Much better.

Going in triumph to the kitchen, Ofelia counted out the money from the change bowl and returned. The little girl surrendered the egg and Ben Warner materialized behind her.

"Heavy transactions," he said.

"My wholesaler. Come in," Luke called, "Blossom-Butt has breakfast on the fire."

Warner hesitated, and Ofelia turned to him expectantly.

"Well, maybe coffee." He came on in. "Coffee, no more," he told her, in Spanish that Luke envied.

"Do you wish Nescoffee, or coffee coffee?"

"No importance." Appreciatively he watched her switch back to the kitchen, then took a fiber chair across from Luke. Ofelia brought in a pot of coffee, along with several sweet rolls. Luke took one and pushed the rest to Warner.

"Help yourself, one's all I can handle."

"Papaya for Señor Huarner?" Ofelia asked.

"How about it?" Luke urged. "It'll only spoil—not that I can tell the difference."

Warner grinned, then helped himself to some. At first glance, only his heavy hornrim glasses saved him from anonymity. One look at him and you could never forget the person beside him. Rugged invisibility, as opposed to rugged individualism. But somehow that golden mean seemed engineered, that placid scaffolding a stall for time. Listening closely, you could detect a sense of harassed activity behind it, as if some monument were being readied for unveiling.

Ofelia came in with the sausage and eggs. "Breakfast also for the señor, *verdad?*"

"No, really, none for me—" Warner began.

"*Verdad.* Look, there's plenty." Luke divided the bowl with him. "She always makes more than I ask for." He frowned at Ofelia in disgust.

She tittered. She'd been instructed to serve double portions whenever Warner dropped by.

"Besides, I say yes to everything when she's around," he said heartily. "Never can tell when I might be passing up La Droit de Señor."

Warner smiled, relaxed, and gently attacked the eggs.

The unexpected guest was never any trouble to the colony, with time and servants so abundant. He was a pleasant excuse for extra cocktails while the kitchen adjusted to his presence. Hospitality usually evened up, of course. But Warner had no way of reciprocating even if he could afford it. His innkeeper—keepress, rather—charged him for whatever meals he had at her pinched posada, didn't for whatever ones he could avoid. The money wasn't much, but neither was the menu, and the decor was a little too realistic for most visitors. Luke guessed the effort it cost Warner to make the rounds of his trap-lines. He concealed it well enough for people to assume he was an unabashed freeloader. But they were mostly willing to admit they'd mind it if he should reform. He was relatively sober as a bartender, relatively discreet for liaisons and feuds, a passable circuit psychiatrist, and a whiz at word games.

As Ofelia cleared the table, Luke lit a Chesterfield and slid the pack across.

"Not my brand."

Luke grinned. "Let me try one of yours."

Lighting the cigarette Warner passed him, he inhaled in surprise. It wasn't quite as bland, but at least it had flavor. Delicados, he'd have to remember.

"I didn't think you could get decent smokes in this country," he said, remembering a weekend in Tijuana. "You sure couldn't years ago."

"Don't you read the billboards?" Warner said. "Mexico is on the march. It'll be the richest country in the world when the next war comes along."

"How do you figure?"

"There won't be any others left."

Luke laughed. "Oh well, the American Colony will carry on, hoisting the flag on the Fourth of July and raffling off sponge cakes for foreign relief."

"You don't think vaporizing the dollar will affect the rate of exchange?"

"Oh, the dollar. Well then, I guess we'll have to switch to pesos like the poor folks."

"How'll we buy them?"

"How do they buy them, Mr. Bones?"

"They don't, they earn them. They're the hired help," Warner said. "We guests aren't permitted to mingle

with the help. They got muscled out of too many of
their own industries that way."

"You mean you can't work here, in a jam?" Luke said
uneasily.

"The law of the land. Unless you're advertising
Camay Soap in Mexico City"—he pronounced it "Cahm-
aye"—"or on a similar cultural mission, you're forced
to be a member of the idle rich."

Luke got a sudden pixy vision of how Warner might
come out on a drawing board, sprawled in those clean
but faded denims of the idle rich. It would be a dig-
nified understatement in forceful black and white,
the wry unkiddable face smiling in no remote attempt
at conviction, as Mr. Benjamin Warner of Zopilotl and
Palm Springs announced for the benefit of his favorite
charity, himself, *I'd walk two miles for a Chesterfield.*

"I miss something?"

"Just thinking," Luke said. "I was with an advertising agency myself. Quit this year, as a matter of
fact."

Warner smiled in bogus understanding. "Found you
were prostituting your talents."

Luke only grinned.

"The rewards of frugality. A chance to pursue your
dreams in Zopilotl. How are you making it—on traveler's checks?" Warner asked abruptly.

"That's right." Luke felt he should be irritated.

"Six months in hell," Warner continued, unruffled,
"to save enough for six months living here in the com-
muter's paradise. Half the people I know are Per-

sephone. The rest of us get by on blackmail. Maury McCoy's got a trust fund set up by his natural father. Victory Richmond gets a little money for Cass's upbringing—"

"Some upbringing," Luke said. "From what I've seen of him, he lives in the streets."

Warner nodded. "Strange kid. Do you know he's never learned to read or write? One time Victory asked him what he learned in school today. Cass said history, and rattled off some anti-gringo propaganda he picked up around the cantinas. Victory can't spell cat in Spanish. So she said, 'That's nice, dear. Now go fetch another jug of rum from Julio's. Mother's going to make a fruitcake.'"

Luke smiled. "And what's your brand of blackmail?"

"She's been working on that fruitcake for the last six years," Warner said. "Me? I have a G.I. pension. A negligible reward for a negligible wound. So you see, we're all remittance men who can't afford the Riviera, any more than we can afford to work for a living. *We're* creative." The word rolled off his tongue with the larded resonance of an old Shakespearean actor's. "A lot of us are artists." He glanced back at Luke's easel. "Adult finger-painters, but we can always call ourselves abstract expressionists. If we're composers, we go in for halftone scales because it's not out of tune that way, it's intentional. As a last resort we're writers."

"What category do you come under?" Luke asked.

"I'm trying to write the great American tragedy."

"How's it coming?"

"Pretty tragic." Warner got up and walked over to the easel. Luke joined him in examining it, trying to see it through his eyes.

It was a nocturnal scene, with stark lighting that emanated from somewhere outside the frame. There was what might have been an old wharf, with a group of hull-like masses occurring through the arbitrary shadows. There was the suggestion of a rotting net, a length of rusty tackle. Then the eye returned to what weren't really boat hulls after all, discovering that the one at the farthest perspective was built from something almost like stone. Another had openings that were never intended to be portholes. Each had a broodingly solid, functional look—although you weren't quite able to recall the function.

"Well, it's certainly professional, anyway," Warner said.

"Don't sound so disappointed."

"I'm always sullen around competence. Has it got a title?"

"How about 'Wharfscape'?"

Warner re-examined it dubiously. "Only God can make a wharf."

"Sure, but you can buy color postcards of *His* stuff for a nickel."

"He's got distribution."

"But not a complete monopoly," Luke insisted. "I was out to make some objects of my own, ones that would have the same positive character as wheels or mattresses—but without being wheels or mattresses. Does it give you a mood, a psychic goose?"

"It disturbs me, anyway. Or maybe I'm just disturbed at being backward. How far am I supposed to go to meet you?"

"Exactly halfway," Luke said. "It's a marriage of the ids. You can't expect me to be entirely responsible to you. You may not be an entirely responsible fellow."

Warner grinned in mock demolishment. "Anyway, it's nice you can work both sides of the street."

He had been drifting toward the door and now, with a lazy flip of his hand, he was gone. "Thanks for breakfast."

The hills, being burned of stubble for the spring planting, seemed steaming in the slant sun, as if freshly risen from the lake. Smoke floated off the steep pitched clearings, giving the air a pearliness and raked-leaf tang of autumn in Missouri. Thoroughly undeceived, Luke dodged through the streets of Zopilotl. There was a car parked somewhere in the vicinity of the plaza, its loudspeaker blasting away at the witching properties of Halo Shampoo. *Champu Halo! El más conocido del mundo!* Intensely perfumed, ensuavens your hair with luster . . . A frantic half-minute hustle, followed by an equally frantic fragment of a ranchero song, the mariachis wounding the air with the soprano yips of new-made castratti.

Bread vendors passed, hands on hips and mincing to keep the flat trays balanced on their heads. Children

trailed them wistfully, awaiting the miracle of a fallen
sugarbun. Both butcher shops were open after a two-
day lull. They stood side by side with their red flags
out, split halves of beef impaled from meat hooks and
dripping. The establishment dogs and cats were
grouped below, competing with each other and the
flies for the puddles, plus whatever dropped to them
by error or intention.

"Luke! *Qué húbole?*"

"*Q'hubo, viejo?*" Luke tossed a wave at Paco, now
Paquito, the diminutive being a sly comment on the
corpulence that comes to anyone who deals in whole
cows. It was also in mimicry of his own abuse of this
diminutive. Everything to Paco had a tender little-
ness: Some of the little stomach, señora? *Tiernito*
when boiled with cabbage, *suavecito* (kissing the
fingers), only one *pesito*.

"Where do you go at such a gallop?" Paco called,
in blood to his elbows as he whicked at a slung rope of
intestines with a machete. Crazy gringos, always in a
hurry.

Up ahead, the second-class Guadalajara bus *Angel
Negro* was discharging passengers. Trucks and buses
had their own names, like ships and horses. This was
called Black Angel because in a previous incarnation
it had transported half a load of souls over a cliff into
paradise. There were more tourists than usual crowd-
ing the slab-width sidewalks, their necks weighted with
cameras like Saint Bernards in search of a snow victim.

At the corner, a gang of kids were playing in the

gutter. They were all Mexicans except, by a techni-
cality, Cass Richmond. Cass couldn't have been more
than four when Victory brought him here. Even so,
he managed to stand out from them, in a convex
rather than a concave way. His reactions were quicker,
his decisions surer; they inevitably gave way to him
in disputes. Realizing that all the other boys were in
their early teens, with anywhere from three to five
years' edge on Cass, Luke wondered how he got to be
their leader.

They'd made a two-lane race course out of pebbles,
and at the moment they were trying to get the idea
over to a pair of beetles. These were the kind that
looked like monstrous cockroaches, with an iridescent
dark green shell from which wings could be extruded.
But they were clumsy insects, requiring an elaborate
takeoff and completely helpless on their backs. The
boys had gotten a loop of thread around a leg of each,
which was used as a leash whenever they got set to fly.

Now Cass yelled *"Ar-r-rancan!"* and there was a wild
scramble as they let the bugs go, jabbing them into
forward motion with twigs or batting them back into
their proper lanes. It was an uneven race, since one
was considerably larger than the other and scuttled
far in front.

"Ya bastante!" Cass called. He took one of the
pebbles and tied it to the large bug's leash as a handi-
cap.

They got set again. But just then the bug made a
rush in the reverse direction. It had gotten up mo-

mentum on the slack thread when the pebble caught and held. Its leg came off, it hit the air for freedom, and the nearest boy swatted it to earth. It lay on its back, oozing some darkish bile and churning its remaining legs like a lazy cyclist. The boys laughed in disgust; one tagged another and they all took out.

All except Cass. He took the thread attached to the small bug, which was frozen in whatever equivalent it had for terror, dragged it over to the large cripple, and tied them together. Then he glanced up the street. A runty cock was conducting forays on the burro-appled cobbles from the safety of his dooryard, darting back at each approach of traffic. As he emerged again Cass whirled the double-weighted thread and let fly. The bugs spatted to the sidewalk short of the cock. He gave a little flap of alarm, hesitated. Then he came strutting forward, setting his feet down on their oiled hinges, lifting them in quick, precise movements.

Both bugs were stationary, the large one possibly dead. The cock halted by it, tipped his head distrustfully. The shadow swept the small bug. It began milling its legs frenziedly. The effort was enough to budge the large bug. Instantly the cock's beak spiked it to the sidewalk. He pecked out its insides leisurely, left the shell, ate half the small bug, and fluffed his wings in satisfaction.

Cass had watched the entire sequence closely, with neither the horrified empathy of a child nor the cynicism of a man. He seemed merely intent on abstracting whatever it could teach him. Now he stooped for a pebble, took aim, and lobbed it at the cock. It bounced harmlessly off his side and he ran squawking back inside. This too had been done without maliciousness. The cock was God to the bug, he was God to the cock, and the natural order hadn't yet succeeded in reversing itself. Then Cass turned to discover Luke behind him.

He waited for Luke to turn into an adult, but Luke's memory wasn't that short.

"Nice shot." He smiled.

Cass smiled back. "Why you reckon that chicken's such a coward?" When he spoke English, it was in the sugared phrasing of his mother.

Luke shrugged. "Too dumb to fight, too smart to try, I guess."

"Some aren't."

"Aren't what? Oh, you mean gamecocks." Luke remembered he was a Missouri man. "Sure, but they're a different breed."

Cass shook his head. "They're still chickens. Why can't they breed together? Mexicans and gringos do."

It was open knowledge that Dionisio Gomez, a shiftless street-singer with a family of his own, was the lover of Victory Richmond.

In embarrassment, still from Missouri in a way he thought he'd gotten over, Luke said: "Well, if they were left alone there probably would be interbreeding. But that way you couldn't keep the strain pure. Chickens, I mean."

"I know." Cass waited politely for elaboration. When none came he said, "Care for a Sidral?"

One man offering to buy another a drink, with the exaggerated casualness of knowing he could be reduced to childhood by the answer.

"Yeah, I could go for a Sidral," Luke said.

He followed the boy across the street to a shop named "The Ancient Pharmacy of Jesus." It had the look of an abandoned basement. Gunnysacks of beans and peanuts were wedged around a drum of kerosene; the shelves burgeoned with an indiscriminate harvest of cans and bottles. Stepping over a coil of rope, Cass rummaged in a lift-top chest labeled MONTEZUMA BEER.

"*Queremos dos Sidrales bien frías*," he told the motionless old man behind the counter, "unless you'd be more partial to a Pepsi, Luke?"

Luke would have preferred a beer to either the synthetic cider or its American cousin, but it was Cass's choice, and his mother was an alcoholic.

"A Sidral's fine," he said.

The old man surfaced from his past long enough to make change. Then Cass took out a bulky knife, pried the caps off, and handed Luke his bottle.

"Thanks. That's some knife you got there." It was one of those Boy Scout Specials he remembered from his childhood, complete with can-openers, corkscrews, and maybe pneumatic drills by now. "Does the rest of your outfit have them?"

"Oh no, not like this." Cass handed it over. "Be careful, it's got a special edge."

Luke tested it, making the proper appreciative sounds, then returned it. They took their drinks to the doorway.

Above the plaza, men in white cottons and women with babies slung in their rebozos were filing back from noon Mass. Cassius watched them with a lean and hungry look, these family people. Squatting, absently grinding the large blade of his superknife on the stone sill, Cass said: "Luke, a chicken like that there—how come he's too smart to fight back?" He spat for lubrication.

Luke laughed. "Well, he winds up in the same pot with the battler. So think of the effort he saves."

"But the ones that win. Don't they save them for —you know, breeding? Like a brave bull, he can have a whole mess of calves."

"That's right," Luke said, awkward at having been taken so literally. "You never lose by trying."

Cass wiped his blade, tested it cautiously with his thumb, then folded and pocketed it. "Mexicans are braver than gringos," he said, "but gringos are richer."

"Well, maybe you'll be both."

"Which is best?"

"I guess that depends." A safe, pointless answer for the young, Luke thought, watching him drain his bottle and sight through it like a telescope. "Either way, people will certainly look up to you."

Cass rose, keeping one hand in his pocket. "Are you a friend of Warner's?"

"Sure, I guess so. Why?"

"Then tell him to quit sleeping with my mother."

He waited alertly, then as he saw that Luke's surprise was genuine, his stance eased.

"Something's going to happen to him if he doesn't quit," he explained.

"What the hell are you talking about?" Luke had no sensible reason for his anger.

Cass merely continued waiting.

"What are you—even if it was true"—Luke broke off in embarrassment.

"It's true." Cass kept his voice steady. "And it's not the same as Dionisio doing it. Dionisio looks up to her."

Now Luke could see the beetle on its back, like a beached ship, leaking bile below a ring of laughing mourners.

"You better tell Warner today," Cass said earnestly.

"All right, I'll tell him."

"*Palabra?* Your word?"

"*Palabra,*" Luke agreed.

The boy sighed and took his hand out of his pocket. "Care for another Sidral? You're more than welcome."

Luke declined it with thanks, set his empty bottle on the sill, and excused himself. Over his shoulder he saw Cass going up the street, balancing himself on a curb where, by squinting, he could shrink the cobbles down to rooftops. It would be good practice, no doubt, in case he ever found himself on top a mile-high catwalk and needed to be brave.

A SENTIMENTAL JOURNEY

*T*hrough rural morning stirrings, as light spread beyond the windshield, last year's convertible rolled the hearsay little towns beneath it. Madera, wine country, with its stubborn vines clenching against another winter. Chowchilla, with a tough old walnut tree standing in the path of progress. Furrows had bypassed it, but now the farmer was tired of such temporizing. He formed a tableau beside it, scratching his head more in awe than anger as he planned his attack. Before they curved from sight Shawn glimpsed a drawn-up truck with a gangsaw and grapples. They were going to pull it down limb by limb, then, like dogs with a bear. Shawn hoped they'd have hard going.

Then Merced, and finally Turlock with its old fruit warehouses haunting the rail siding. Shawn asked directions of a cheerful morning constitutionalist, and at 8 A.M. he turned in the graveled drive beside a cocked tin mailbox stenciled KAIN.

There was the rambling frame house he'd seen by snapshot, bordered with greek fire bushes. The garden, mostly abandoned tomato plants, had reverted to the gophers. Young trees drooped from their stakes on the path to three long chicken houses. From the center one Elroy poked his head out, waved, ducked back in. There was a flurry of desperate squawks as he reappeared with a bleating chicken. Grabbing it beneath the head with one hand, setting the other at the base of its neck, he stretched vigorously and threw it from him. The chicken clung to the air a second, wings pumping, then hit the ground at a yawing run, its long neck dangling like a sudden swan's.

Shawn watched his cousin coming toward him, heavier-set than himself and darker. There seemed in Elroy little of his aunt Olivia, Shawn's mother, in the chromosomes they shared: only the stamp of his father, Shawn's Uncle Benjamin, the blunt will riding through the plasm. They shook hands self-consciously.

"Hope you didn't kill the old red rooster just on my account, Roy."

"No, I been culling some pullets. That one had a digestive screwup; couldn't put on any meat." He grinned as Shawn watched the chicken, twitching like an epileptic. "Very scientific, same principle as hanging. Don't worry, it's plenty dead." He slapped Shawn's arm lightly. "Well, you're still making out in Hollywood. New buggy, clothes, and everything."

"None of it'll look new by the time it's paid for."

Elroy nodded without belief. "I hardly dress up anymore. Too bagged at night, and the town's dead. How's the wife?"

"Okay, thanks. How's Hattie?"

His cousin shrugged. "She's catching a nap, they'll call us when he starts to go. Can't be much longer. Like to take a look around the plant?"

Shawn trailed him down the slope past a compost pile to the chicken houses. Stepping gingerly between the droppings and the chalky feed sacks, he followed the evolution from the brooder where chicks milled like fat idiot canaries, through the pinfeather stage in which they resembled pubescent vultures, down to the finishing house. Here the clamor had a tenor quality, the bickering drew blood. Elroy made a sudden dive for a hen, hoisted it aloft and prodded its breast. It pecked him hysterically between hoarse screams. Elroy laughed and slapped its head affectionately, temporarily paralyzing it.

"Beauty? This one'll go three pounds if it's an ounce," he said, stroking the hen while it waited behind glazed eyes, as if quietly sharing his pride.

It looked about average to Shawn, though it seemed the pick of the flock. "Sure, Roy. Nice."

"You know, if a guy could get a little ahead," he said, "just enough to fix up a killing room and hire some part-time help, he could eliminate the middleman. Birds like these're worth lugging to Bakersfield direct."

"Why Bakersfield?"

"Hell, man, that's where I live. I was assistant manager of Shop-Rite, remember? I could unload everything I got on them alone. Besides, my girl's there."

Shawn smiled. "Besides."

"How about it? Want to put your loose change to work? Pay a damn sight better interest than the Beverly Hills branch of the Bank of America."

"Cheviot Hills, unfortunately. And it's the other way around," Shawn said awkwardly, "the bank owns me, skin and soul. Otherwise I would in a minute, Roy."

Elroy sighed and let the hen dangle. "They were just about to open Shop-Rite Number Two when the old man got laid up. Guess who would have taken over as manager of Number One. That's all Faye and I were waiting for," he said. "Then I had to come up here, try to make this dump break even. I haven't heard from her in three months. Guess she got tired waiting for *this* to pay out."

He swung his arm in a savage, inclusive gesture. The hen, snapped out of its coma, set up a great squawking and flapping to get free. Elroy jerked his arm back and hurled the thing. It sailed out over the flock in a wobbly trajectory, landing on the back of a cockerel. Instantly, the entire chicken house became insane with fright. Each bird tried to climb the back nearest it, clawing in frenzy to escape the terror from above. The air shook with the sound of rusty winches. Then, through the settling snowfall of feathers, they gradually began unknotting themselves, moving off stiffly to bunch in ruffled clusters. In the center of the floor, where a dozen-odd lay smothered, there was dead calm.

Elroy stood hammering his thigh lightly with his fist. "Christ, it's a pleasure to wring their necks! Of all the filthy, dung-eating animals in existence, he had to pick on these to raise. My father, the country squire. *He* wouldn't raise them in batteries to save space and keep them off their own litter. That crowded them, that wasn't *humane*. And when they all came down with coxy he wouldn't write the state farm advisor. Hell, what's a little thing like fifty percent mortality if it saves dealing with a *bureaucrat*? God *damn* these directives from the sickbed," he said. "He'll probably tell the undertaker how to embalm him." He turned away, letting it drain out of him while Shawn waited uncomfortably.

When he turned back he was all right again. "Maybe I should invest in your racket. Think I'd have a chance in motion pictures?"

"Well, there's a couple of approaches," Shawn said. "One of them is to learn Hungarian."

"By God, with this monk's life I been leading I'm almost ready for the other approach. Let's go check in at the house."

They let themselves inside the parlor quietly. The drapes were drawn. Through the gloom Shawn could distinguish his Aunt Hattie, dozing in the couch against the flowered wall. As he stood hesitantly, her eyes opened directly on him.

"Yes, dear?" She blinked, sat upright with an uncertain laugh. "I must have been dreaming. Oh my, let me look at you."

They met in a clumsy embrace. She was smaller than he'd remembered, her voice and features like those of a half-accurate impersonation.

"You've gained weight," she said in approval. "Don't you think he's gained a little, son?"

"Yeah," Elroy said. "Is there any coffee?"

"I'll go make a fresh pot. That's all he lives on," she told Shawn, "the blacker the better." She shuddered in emphasis. "At least if he could take a little cream and sugar in it. How is Virginia?"

"On a diet," Shawn said without thinking. "That is, a special high-calorie diet."

The kitchen was like the negative of some mislaid photo, its familiarity thrusting through its transposed values. While the sink was not the sink of adolescence, the cast iron skillet above it was, and the quilted potholders. The figured oilcloth on the shelves still impended above Aunt Hattie grilling waffles for the cousins on a lucent summer morning, while Uncle Benjamin defended agnosticism (and lost a customer) in the basement workshop. Now with Uncle Benjamin dropping so neatly from the Christmas list, going down for the third stroke as his nephew watched objectively from the shore, Shawn wondered if the old man would remain as willfully ignorant of death as he had been of reality.

In the first world war the entire army, with the exception of a second lieutenant named Benjamin Kain, had somehow been out of step. When neither would acknowledge error, the numerically superior disputant sent Buck Private Kain to Texas to break mules to harness for the cavalry. Upon armistice, perhaps in polar revulsion, Benjamin and a partner moved to Bakersfield, California, to start a horseless-carriage agency. The car they handled was the Kissell Gold Bug Speedster, a luxurious open two-seater that the agricultural community could easily afford to forgo. The partner sold out, and after an undramatic struggle ascended to some vague, strategic post at General Motors. Benjamin, however, clung to the Kissell so tenaciously that he drew a letter from the Hartford home office commending him for his faith, his energy, and his myopia in reading the handwriting on the wall. A month after he married, he was bankrupt.

Benjamin had married Hattie, the less flighty of a brace of indigent sisters. The same year Olivia married a quiet older diabetic who was a good amateur chef, because of his special diet, and a good amateur investor, because he bet the market to continue rising indefinitely. His stock tips enabled brother-in-law Benjamin to pay off his creditors to the last scrupulous penny by the time the crash came. Olivia's husband (by then Shawn's father), who had smelled a tinge of vinegar in that winy October air and mentioned it in vain to Benjamin, was only partially wiped out.

The day Shawn started school Olivia bought a baby grand. They both began taking lessons, fellow conspirators against the heavy-footed, habit-ridden world of Father's. They practiced together, improved their minds with radio concerts, dreamed of the day when they would play duets by candlelight in a setting in which Father was never quite accounted for. But soon it became evident that Shawn was a child prodigy. He improved so much faster than Mother that she could only share his gifts as a spectator, encouraging him to be sensitive and truly free. She filled this role with dedication till the following year, when she ran away to Mexico with the piano teacher.

Father contributed what he could to Shawn's upkeep when Uncle Benjamin and Aunt Hattie took him in. But even this shaky income would have quickly been absorbed by the sanitarium from which Father emerged on decreasing visits, each time looking more wasted and unfamiliar. Shawn's only memory of the funeral was his impatience to return to the tree house he was building with his cousin Elroy.

Sometime later, when Shawn could be alluded to as an orphan and had secretly manufactured a romantic death for Mother at the hands of revolutionists, a package arrived. It was shortly after his birthday. There was a Mexican postmark on it, with no return address. It contained some kind of doll with black Latin eyes, and though he was long past the age for it Shawn took to bringing it to bed with him. He would conduct whispered conversations with it, this nocturnal confessor to whom he'd look for signs and dispensations like a father's. Othertimes he'd heap it with indulgences as if it were a lost puppy, or a son.

It wasn't that he wasn't treated well; he wasn't treated equally. His shortcomings were excused and his successes magnified on the grounds of artistic temperament. As bemused custodians of the flame, his aunt and uncle felt obliged to continue his piano lessons when they could least afford to. (Benjamin was barely weathering the Depression with a radio sales & service shop. Since he insisted on describing the merchandise as he saw it and limiting the repairs to what were needed, his sales were negligible and his services were mostly free.) But when Shawn got to high school, it was easier to reach girls through the blues than the Bach Inventions, easier to find the money for the girls he'd reached by playing in non-union gin mills, instead of joining Elroy in an early-morning paper-route. Besides, in experiencing the stale late hours and the cadged drinks, he could feel he was working out his genes. When that phase ended, he was going to win a scholarship to Juilliard and become George Gershwin. His teachers said he couldn't miss. Instead, he graduated from Bakersfield High six months after Pearl Harbor and was enrolled in World War II.

Between fact and potential lies a vacuum known as war. Its major occupations are sitting and comparing the past with the future. Like most veterans, Shawn

came home resolved to make sense out of this next
half of his life. He took a studio apartment in Hollywood within walking distance of Sunset and Vine and
signed up for a course in music theory on the G.I. Bill.
Lugging mortar shells hadn't been the supplest disci-
pline for his fingers, but he was still a pretty fair party
pianist. He had enough presentability to meet people
who could give him a hand up, and when the night
was far enough along they usually would volunteer to.
Nothing quite ever came of it, but the possibility was
exciting. And there was excitement in the sheer hard
work of writing an exercise in canons that would satisfy
the professor (a brilliant refugee who was looking for
studio orchestrating himself). *Good*, the old boy would
say, *now tear it up, forget it. That was only one solu-
tion. Don't use it again till you learn others. Taste is
choice, and a man with one trick has no choice.*

But five years later he was at the end of the ladder.
He'd climbed there like a monkey on a stick, leaving
aspects of himself behind: the concert artist, the good
jazz piano man, the serious composer who hadn't found
himself in time in a profession where you had to be as
young as Mozart to be in the running, and wait as long
as Bartok to be heard. He was now in the assembly
line that shuttles music from the inspiration or night-
rising of the creator or producer's nephew, past the
arranger who makes it plausible, the transcriber who
makes it playable, down to the studio musicians who,
stuck with it, present it to the great American ear as
innocuously as their collective conscience or union re-

hearsal fees permit. He had married Ginny, partly because a man with a Home to protect is a man without
funny viewpoints, partly because he wanted to. Uncle
Benjamin, whom the war years had bailed out, had
plunged his entire savings in a chicken ranch upstate,
and three years ago he had his first stroke.

The illusion flickered out. The light was the grey
real light of circa now, illuminating none of them with
youth or confidence or common purpose. Hattie set
the coffee out, along with some burnt scraped toast.
By her wary manner, Shawn gathered that his uncle's
room lay directly off the kitchen. She bit into a slab
of toast, set it down with a bewildered look.

"He's only sixty-five," she said. "Why, people don't
even start retiring these days till then." Her veined
hand strayed absently to her brittle hair, then came
away self-consciously. She looked to Shawn for proof
that actuary tables couldn't lie.

"He always drove himself pretty hard," he said.

But she wasn't listening. "All week long, he's barely
eaten enough to keep a mouse alive." It was the only
explanation. How could anything run down if it were
kept in fuel? "Goodness, I'd almost forgotten—after
a drive like that Shawn must be ravenous. I'll scramble us all some eggs."

"Mother," Elroy said patiently, "Shawn didn't drop
in for breakfast."

"I know, dear. I just thought, while Dad's sleeping,
that we might—"

"He isn't sleeping. He's dying."

Hattie smiled brightly in embarrassment. Shawn got to his feet. "Is there somewhere I could sort of look in at him?"

Elroy pointed, and as Shawn started toward the door his aunt said, "If he's awake, see if he won't take a nice hot cup of broth."

He smiled noncommittally, closed the door on Elroy's grunt of disgust and found himself in a hallway off a partly-opened door. A man was seated at the foot of the bed. He sprang up and hurried out.

"You're the nephew," he said cordially. "I'm Dr. Fisher." He caught Shawn's hand and shook it, cocked forward as if habitually embarrassed by his height. In his late fifties, he was carrying a book in which he kept one finger as a marker.

"How is he, doctor?"

"Much better," Dr. Fisher said. "I believe he just might pull through. The next few days will tell the story. Come along, now, he's had enough company."

Shawn let himself be steered back to the kitchen in a confusion of emotions: disgust at his worthless trip, then at himself for his lack of elation.

Hattie looked up hopefully as they entered.

"He's resting," Dr. Fisher announced. "My reading seems to have relaxed him. We'll have to let the Lord spell me for awhile."

Shawn took another look, as Elroy began grinning. "Is that a Bible you're carrying, doctor?"

"It is," Dr. Fisher chuckled, "and my practice is confined to medicating the spirit."

"It will be," Elroy said, "when he gets his doctor's ticket."

Hattie frowned at him. "Now you know that's just a formality. Not that Dr. Fisher isn't perfectly legal already in some states," she told Shawn.

"The doctor is going to perform at the funeral," Elroy said.

"Well, let's hope that won't be for a good while yet," Fisher said, a little testily.

Again Shawn felt out of phase, lagged by his reactions. Now he had to reaccept Uncle Benjamin's passing—not shored by his prejudices but frightened and vulnerable to what he'd always branded an anthology of myths. It intensified the loss, somehow.

"I think I'll take a look at him," Shawn said.

"I wouldn't recommend that, young man," Fisher began. "We don't want him too exhausted for the evening meditations—"

Shawn closed the kitchen door on the rest of it. After a pause, then a murmured inquiry from Hattie, Fisher resumed resonantly.

"Why yes, Mrs. Kain, we certainly owe it to ourselves to preserve our strength. Make mine sunny side up . . ."

Shawn stepped inside the death room. Uncle Benjamin lay straight and perfectly still. Unshaven this early, his overnight's growth of bristle made his hollow features even more eroded. The left eye was partially open, glazed and unseeing, already the eye of a corpse. Then Shawn realized that the whole side was paralyzed.

The feeling he had had of seeing the house and all its occupants as reflections in a fun-house mirror was augmented, probably by his fatigue. Even the old brass bedstead remained familiar but distorted, until Shawn remembered it as his own.

He sat down beside it weakly, drawing level with the tenant who had dispossessed him. Here he had journeyed through his adolescence, reading *Spicy Detective Tales* and *Flying Aces* in the long spring nights that ached with imminence. Of the twin mysteries, love, like prosperity, had been just around the corner, and death was something that could never touch him. They would merge, just before he fell asleep, and if he had an emission it would be connected with invulnerability and flying. He would be in a World War Spad, trailing a Fokker as it fell in flames. Zooming down and gliding level with it, he would pull his wing-tip close to his antagonist's and gallantly call, "Climb aboard. . . ."

But now such acrobatics were too late for both of them. Benjamin would never have let go of the joystick and abandoned himself to love and trust in someone else's strength. It had taken Fisher the minister to pull the self-made man out of death-long pigheaded tailspin and win him to everlasting life. It must have been the only argument the old man ever lost, Shawn thought, absently watching the coverlet begin to rise and fall.

He stood up quickly, started to call them from the

kitchen. Then Uncle Benjamin's right eye opened, the right side of his mouth smiled.

"Play the piano," he said.

"Yes, sir?" Shawn asked.

"Play the piano," he repeated thickly, negotiating the syllables with a drunk's precision.

"There's no piano here, sir."

His uncle's smile vanished, replaced by his expression of contempt for weakness.

"What would you like to hear?" Shawn said, deciding to humor him.

"Get out."

Shawn hesitated in the old despair and anger.

"Or talk sense," Uncle Benjamin said. "You've studied long enough." His chest labored. "When are you going to give a concert?"

"I wasn't good enough," Shawn told him.

"You quit."

Stung by the flat rejection, Shawn said, "I just didn't have it."

"You quit," came the relentless, self-appointed voice of conscience.

"All *right*, I quit. We can't all be successes. You quit selling Kissell Gold Bug Speedsters, didn't you?"

Uncle Benjamin laughed harshly, in his favorite element once more. "I didn't quit the Kissell. It quit me."

The look of righteousness (though only half of it was there) that had lain between them like a wall for half Shawn's lifetime drove him to a fury of demolishment.

"Uncle Benjamin, aren't you *ever* wrong? Can't I accidentally be right just once?"

There was no answer.

"God damnit," Shawn said, "at least they didn't bust me to buck private in *my* war!"

In horror, he saw the old man slowly heave himself erect on his right elbow. "You? You couldn't pour piss from a cavalry boot if the directions were written on the heel!"

Then as they all ran in from the kitchen, he painfully swung his right arm up from the bedcovers. Leveling it at Fisher, who stood cocked forward with a yolky, gape-mouthed look, he said: "I'm through being your guinea pig. Go scout heaven for yourself!" As Shawn bent to ease him beneath the covers, Uncle Benjamin flung him aside. "There *is* no heaven, you superstitious nincompoop." Laughing weakly, he fell back on the pillow. "There is a hell, however," he said in relish.

When the doctor that Elroy phoned for—the M.D.—reached to take his pulse, the old man roused for the final time. Sweeping his assembled kinfolk with his one good eye, he said,

"Gee-up there, you ornery bastards—we got a load to move!"

Then the engine which had driven him for sixty-five years commenced to race. It was just a question of time, which Shawn couldn't spare, till it tore loose from its housing.

Twelve hours after leaving Cheviot Hills, twenty-seven hours after he'd last risen from the bed he shared with Ginny (spicier than old detective tales, and as addicting), Shawn shot back through Chowchilla where a hamstrung tree lay on its back, its walnut stump revving like a heart, perhaps, pumping two hundred eighty times a minute as it drove sap into the vacuum of its lopped limbs in a last crazed effort to put forth green leaves. It didn't know it didn't have it anymore. But then a tree has no capacity for self-analysis; nor can it mourn.

BLOOD HARVEST

At the woman's moan—a rising note of alarm—Jose Maria woke and rocked her shoulder gently but insistently. Her features relaxed as she rolled over on her back. Her breathing was regular again, part of the same small noises of the night. The serape had slipped partway free. She lay in her undergown beneath the narrow moonlight, black braids glistening against the straw mat, her belly seven months full. Jose Maria set his palm against it in undiminished wonder.

His woman smiled, her eyes remaining closed. "I dreamed."

"I know," he said.

"It was a heavy dream."

"But it has passed," he said.

Sighing, she placed her hand above his, bulkily turning to face him. Her belly met the soothing pressure of his palm like a horse's muzzle. After fourteen barren years together, this thing could happen. Thanks to the final heed of several saints—one could never be too sure where credit lay—and Tia Caridad, the witch woman.

"There was a great bird, in my dream," the woman told him.

"A bird?" Jose Maria asked, listening to his old ox snuffle in its sleep beneath the patio shed.

"A great sleek bird, all of black. He kept circling and circling, as if in search of something . . ."

"He was a crow, in hunger of new corn."

"Do you think so?" she said anxiously. "You must guard the seedlings well."

"I only joke. The field is not yet broken."

"Still, there is no dream without a meaning."

He nodded uneasily. "I will keep a sharp eye. Now let us sleep, the day is almost here."

She yawned in agreement, and soon her belly rose and fell in the firm tidal rhythm that no man could hasten, as one more night toward fatherhood went wheeling under.

The speckled cock crowed prematurely from his roost above the ox. Jose Maria smiled, thinking of the many chicks sprung from its loins, even this least beast, from the many hens that it had trod. Yes, of eggs and chickens, of a serviceable ox to till his field and of the

woman he had wived to share its harvest, he had sufficiency. And with the child to be, no lack would remain.
Son or daughter, he assured himself, it had no importance. At this late date, in his gratitude there was
no room for greed.

Nevertheless a son, should Tia Caridad discern one
in her castings, would cause sufficiency to be abundance. Then let any thieving bird whichever do its
worst.

With the first light, Jose Maria urged the rheumy ox
out to the common acreage. He had fallen behind
schedule, owing to an injury he'd received while clearing bramble. Tough and fire-resistant, it had deflected
his *hijo* of a machete into his right ankle. The fields
of all his neighbors had received their preliminary
plowing, and were only waiting for the final one pre-
ceding sowing. His own plot, gaunt with blackened
stubble, was but a quarter furrowed. Much industry
was due before the rains came. Hitching the wooden
plow to his ox, Jose Maria called out *Arre, buey!* and
began hobbling in its wake. Slow as the old brute
was, it was painful to keep pace.

The sun was strongly in ascent when a drift of dust
came up the distant road. On fiesta days, people sometimes journeyed down it to sell excess hides or produce
in the valley, or to make purchases for the adventure
of it; but there were seldom visitors here to the plateau.
Jose Maria paused, curious to see who might have
traffic with the pueblo.

A burro plodded into view, heavily laden, with a tall man following behind. Every little while the man would leave the road to wander in the unworked land that bordered it, peering and stooping eagerly. He had the air of a water diviner's apprentice. Discovering Jose Maria against the corrugated landscape, he waved energetically. Jose Maria returned the greeting and roused the ox back into motion. Then the stranger made his way across the fields to him.

"*Buenos días!* Very warm, is it not?"

For the sake of politeness, Jose Maria agreed that it was warm. He watched the other man remove his eyeglasses and wipe them with a bandana. Light of hair and complexion, his appearance was as unfamiliar to this region as his speech. Probably some Mexican from farther north whose blood, unlike an Indian's, was of who knew what mixtures.

Now the stranger produced machine-made cigarettes. Jose Maria accepted one, together with a light, and touched his forehead in thanks.

"*Qué tierra tan hermosa!*" the stranger gestured expansively at the horizon. "How handsome a land—and how old and unchanged!"

Rolling the bland, tasteless smoke over his palate, Jose Maria waited uncertainly. Surely no portion of the earth had been created earlier than another.

"And you have been here such a long time."

"All my life," Jose Maria said in surprise.

The stranger laughed. "No, your people, your race.

Fíjese, I am a student of your history. Do you understand?"

Jose Maria nodded restlessly. Few Mexicans he'd seen made sense.

"I have come to search your ruins for your past. There must be many ruins hereabout, true?"

"Who knows?" Conversing in riddles was doubly tiring. Jose Maria squatted, easing the pain in his foot which was beginning to radiate to his calf.

Kneeling quickly in concern, the stranger asked: *"Hombre, qué paso?"*

"I cut myself. A foolish accident, it is nothing."

"What have you on the wound?"

"Various remedies." The cure was of Tia Caridad's devising. First there had been heated she-goat dung to draw the poison, followed by unguents known to her alone.

The stranger grimaced at the incrusted bandage. "Wait here."

He hurried toward his burro who, finding nothing worth the eating at the roadside, had trailed after him. A gully lay between them, and as he crossed it something caught the stranger's eye. He scooped it up, studying it every which way before pocketing it. Then he returned with a leather sack and a canteen.

"When did this happen?" He removed the stained clout and cast it aside.

"A week past. Perhaps two."

"And it has not begun to heal?"

"No," Jose Maria admitted, with a sense of disloyalty toward the witch woman. "But it has not worsened."

Shaking his head, the stranger washed Jose Maria's foot with soap as well as water. His touch was sure and gentle. Then he bathed the raw inflamed gash with a fluid that foamed and stung, afterwards anointing it with balsam from a tube, and bound the whole with clean gauze.

"If that had gone much longer, you could have lost a foot."

Since such events were of God's will and no one else's, Jose Maria merely shrugged politely. He thanked the stranger nevertheless and introduced himself.

"I am called Brady," the other man responded.

"Much pleasure, señor Bredi."

"The pleasure is mine."

Now, trying to appear casual, señor Bredi handed him the object he'd discovered in the gully. "Do you recognize who this is?"

Jose Maria smiled and shook his head. It was a crudely shaped clay figurine, half the length of a man's hand. Perhaps a child's toy at one time. Such debris could still be turned up by the plow.

"It is not Tl——, the god of fertility?"

And as señor Bredi named this Name forbidden by the priest, pronouncing it correctly in the Old Tongue, Jose Maria stared at him intently.

"How do you know these things?"

"I told you," señor Bredi laughed, "I am interested

in learning more about your ancestors. I have come from far off for this purpose."

"From the Capital?" The government would not be welcome here, if all that he had heard of it were true.

"No, *hombre*, farther yet. I have nothing to do with Mexico City. I am a North American."

Jose Maria began relaxing. The pursuits of *norteamericanos* were reported to be lacking in both harm and logic.

As he returned the figurine señor Bredi asked him, "Can you tell me where I might encounter others like this?"

"They could be anywhere beneath your feet, señor."

"But not one section more than others?"

Jose Maria hesitated, then nodded reluctantly toward the nearby hill that no one ever cultivated.

From the plowing below, he could follow señor Bredi scrambling up the slope, digging spaced shallow holes. He does no harm, Jose Maria repeated to himself, and undoubtedly his curiosity will be exhausted soon. But when he started homeward for his midday meal (he did not want the woman bringing it this far in her condition), he saw, with an unreasonable feeling of disquietude, that the North American had pitched a canvas lean-to at the base. And at the very crown of the abode of the Old Ones, he had staked out a scar-shaped area for excavation.

Señor Bredi was waiting for him at the half-plowed plot the following morning. "How goes it, my friend?"

"It goes well, thanks," Jose Maria answered. "And with yourself?"

"Less well. Would you like coffee?"

"It is not a *molestia*?"

"None. It is already made."

The tall northerner led him to his camp site, filled a tin cup from a blackened pot that nestled in the embers. He sat sucking at a pipe, his bony, restless face half-hidden in the shadows so that Jose Maria seemed to see the skull's frank grin beneath it.

"How is the foot?"

"Better, I believe." So much so, he realized, that he'd been unaware of it till now.

"Good. Do nothing to it, let it rest," señor Bredi said absently. Then he sat forward, tense with excitement. "Jose, I found part of another idol yesterday, a large one. But I am sure it is the same god. I think he must have had his temple here. I need you to help me dig for it."

"*Dispénseme, señor.* I cannot help you," Jose Maria said quickly. "I have my crop to ready."

"But it would take a few days only. And I would pay you at the rate of five pesos."

The offer was a fair one. If it had been presented at another time, and if the digging were for other purposes. . . . He shook his head regretfully.

"You understand I meant five pesos daily."

"Daily, señor?"

For answer, señor Bredi rose and ducked into the lean-to, reappearing with a five-peso coin. He lobbed it at Jose Maria who plucked it from the air, bouncing its good heft in his palm. Paper money had its utility, no doubt, for those who could guard it properly. But honest silver such as this, hidden anywhere, would remain till it was needed, unharmed by fire, insects, mould, or any other theft of nature. One would have to be a rich man or a fool to spurn such wages. Why, then, did his discomfort persist?

Shaking it from him with a sigh, Jose Maria said: "Very well, señor. Let us dig."

When he returned with the ox at midday his woman held her tongue, sensing his preoccupation. But by afternoon any misgivings were gone. Señor Bredi's earlier find had been pure luck. The ancient hill was clearly going to yield no secrets. But the digging, aside from its futility, was easier than plowing. And certainly the company of a fellow soul was more congenial than that of an ox.

"These *figuras* that you seek, señor," Jose Maria asked cautiously, "these statues—are they of value?"

"For me, much value."

"Have you none in your own land?"

Señor Bredi laughed. "We have only new things, all created by machinery and each like the other."

"What then does one do with his old possessions?"

"He exchanges them for new ones."

Jose Maria smiled. At least such falsehoods helped to pass the time.

"You will be the same way soon, Jose. Your leisure

will vanish, your customs be forgotten—all in the name of progress. You will have machines for slaves, and you will become in turn a slave to them."

"I, señor?"

Señor Bredi gestured wearily at the landscape. "All of Mexico. Your government will see to it."

"Ah, the government," Jose Maria nodded in uneasy respect. It could command all men and institutions—even the church, if it so chose. It could levy taxes, conscript one's sons, set law and order to one side, and it was said to track transgressors down and try them on the spot. It was a force he did not understand.

"Courage, man," señor Bredi laughed, "this will not happen overnight."

Jose Maria bent to his spade again. *"Gracias á Diós!"*

At day's end they stood thigh-deep in nothing, surrounded by a pile of dirt. But señor Bredi seemed content, which was of course his privilege.

"Well, Rome was not constructed in one day," he said cheerfully, as they shared a flask of his mezcal.

"Claro qué no," Jose Maria agreed. "Nor China reached."

Warmed equally by liquor and the rich variety of nonsense in the universe, he strolled back to his hut. A neighbor was seated with his woman, sipping manzanilla tea.

"How goes it, señora Prieto?"

The neighbor shrugged, flipping her palm in a seesaw motion. *"Así, así.* And with yourself, Jose Maria?"

"Very busily, of late. I am assisting the señor Bredi

in his work," he announced casually. "It is not everyone who can be sympathetic with the North American
temperament, and the responsibilities are many."

As expected, both females set up a clamor of questioning but he waved it aside. "What we are doing
does not easily lend itself to understanding." To divert
their disappointment he turned to his woman. "Have
the animals been fed?"

"Of corn and leavings both. How fares your foot?"
she said anxiously. "No better?"

Glancing down in pleased surprise, Jose Maria set
his weight upon it. The pain was but an echo now.
Laughing in relief his woman hurried to remove the
bandage. Except for a knitting scar, the foot was as
unblemished as a baby's.

"Profound are the ways of Tia Caridad," señora
Prieto murmured.

His woman nodded. "I must send her a clutch of
eggs."

"Tia Caridad? That mountain of inertia?" Jose
Maria said disgustedly. "Hers is the profoundness of
a starved sow at the slop basin." The mezcal had set
his tongue to swinging freely, and he enjoyed the con-
sternation it produced. "It was señor Bredi's skill that
made me well again."

"*De veras?*" señora Prieto asked weakly.

"For a certainty. Among the North Americans, there
is no guessing in these matters."

When the neighbor had left, Jose Maria's woman

faced him timidly. "Is it wise to speak this way of Tia Caridad?"

"When one has wealth, one has no need for wisdom." She smiled. "Are we so wealthy then, my husband?"

"Can you doubt it, swollen like the belly of a sail?"

And as the woman dropped her eyes in pleased embarrassment, Jose Maria held her to him, self-conscious in the clear but failing light of day. In his pocket, the five-peso piece was a reminder that, as faith breeds miracles, wealth breeds wealth.

The second morning of employ his spade struck something. Señor Bredi instantly took over, tenderly freeing it from the soil with the aid of a hand broom. It was a chunk of earthenware. Jose Maria watched him crouching raptly, easing additional shards to light. Assembled, they would form no more than half a water jug. For yesterday's five pesos, let alone the ones to come, he could have bought a burro load of new jugs. About this time they noticed the señora Prieto waiting patiently below, with an infant slung in her rebozo.

"*Quién es ella?*" señor Bredi asked.

"It is a neighbor," Jose Maria told him, starting to wave her away.

"No, let us see what she wants."

They made their way down the hill to her and, emboldened, señora Prieto thrust her baby forward.

"His food is of no use to him," she said, without preliminaries. "It passes through him like a sieve. *Sale puro líquido!*"

Señor Bredi nodded sympathetically, asked a few questions and fetched some tablets from his lean-to. Dissolving one in water, he helped señora Prieto coax it down, then gave her others with instructions for their use. He also told her what the baby might and might not eat.

"And what do I owe the señor? He must remember that I am a widow."

"You owe me nothing," señor Bredi smiled.

"Señor, I am not so poor I cannot pay."

"Nor am I so poor I cannot share."

"Then thanks," she said flatly. "We shall see if the remedy serves."

"She lacks in confidence as well as culture, that one," Jose Maria said sadly.

Late that afternoon a little girl called shyly to them, and señor Bredi sent him down to see her. He returned with a half a chicken wrapped in a banana leaf.

"A present," he said.

Señor Bredi rubbed his hands in pleasure. "A banquet! Thank God I need not suffer canned sardines again tonight. Who was that?"

"The aunt of the baby of the evil stomach."

"*Mejor que mejor.* The medicine must have worked."

"Of course it worked," Jose Maria said in surprise. "Why should it not work?"

In the days succeeding, a woman with the ague appeared, another with a child who had been bitten by a scorpion, a hollow-chested boy who when he spat, spat blood, and a blacksmith subject to the fits. Some were quickly healed by señor Bredi, others he declared to be beyond the aid of anyone in the locality. Jose Maria shared the surprise of those who asked how such ability could be so variable. Señor Bredi finally lost his patience after Eliseo Fuentes and his brother brought their uncle to the camp site on a litter. The old man had been unable to walk ever since his stallion kicked him.

"When did this happen?" the señor asked, examining him.

"Two harvests past, *maestro.*"

"You err to call me master. Is there no sensation in this limb at all?"

"None."

"Nor here?"

"Neither."

"Then you require an operation. And even this may not restore you."

The old man crossed himself. "I am ready, *maestro.* Serve yourself to proceed."

"No, no. You require surgery."

"*Como?*"

"A hospital, man!"

The elder nephew sidled forward. "Perhaps the señor can devise some poultice made of *sangre de caballo,* with certain other potions of his knowledge."

"*Horse* blood?" señor Bredi asked, as if the suggestion had been idle. "How could this serve for anything?"

"The injury was inflicted by a horse, señor. Naturally, it is part of the remedy we have been using."

"*Válgame Diós!* Who put such ideas in your heads?"

All three kept silent in embarrassment. Then Jose Maria spoke up uncomfortably:

"There is a woman here who deals with such things."

"Ah, now I understand," the señor Bredi said with an odd, almost angry satisfaction. "I am well acquainted with her type. Her prices are very dear, but there is no infirmity she cannot cure, true?"

"*Sí, señor,*" the old man and his nephews murmured.

"The cure may take a lifetime, but it always works."

"*Sí, señor.*"

"And if it does not work, the fault is someone else's."

They nodded uncertainly.

"Well, she is wrong about one thing. It is not a horse's blood which you require. It is his droppings—"

"*Sí, señor?*" Their faces brightened.

"—to replace whatever brains you have!" señor Bredi told them in a fury of disgust. "She is a thief, this woman. She is worse than a thief, for in the end she steals hope as well as health, and you are madmen if you listen to her."

While his compadres stared at the ground in sullen confusion, Josa Maria stood by uneasily. To accuse Tia Caridad of occasional human weakness was one thing, but words like these were something else.

"A village as remote as this should have a doctor," señor Bredi continued, quiet and persuasive. "You need but write the Capital and they will send one. It will be some student serving his apprenticeship, but better far than nothing. True?"

The old man nodded vaguely from his litter. "This may be," he said politely. "But to our disgrace señor, no man in the pueblo has the mastery of writing."

"The writing will be mine. You need but fix your marks to it. Agreed?"

Hovering eagerly, his arms tucked stiffly at his sides like folded wings, señor Bredi blinked behind his eyeglasses.

The old man smiled up at him. "We will talk of it among ourselves," he said.

On the way home, Jose Maria was halted by a hoarse cry. He turned to see El Rano squatting near a ditch behind him. Some said he lived in swamps and ditches, and on evenings in the frog season his voice could be distinguished in their croakings. He had the appearance of a frog as well, and lacked both human speech and intelligence. Tia Caridad employed him as her eyes and ears, for she could communicate with him in some way. She also used him as her summoner.

"Does the señora wish to see me?"

El Rano's arms thrashed hingelessly from his misshapen torso. Then uttering his dismal, urgent cry once more, he leaped across the ditch and went bounding off into the dusk.

In nervous excitement Jose Maria hurried to the witch woman's hut. It stood by itself at the head of a narrow cobbled street. When the door was shut no one might enter, but now it lay ajar.

"Señora?" he called, and when no one bid him differently he stepped inside.

Somewhere in the darkness there was a sense of presence, vast and waiting. Then as his eyes adjusted to the faint glow of a brazier, the bulky outline of Tia Caridad emerged. Imprisoned in her flesh, she sat with a serape draped around her, eyes sunk from view within her doughy features. He had never seen her otherwise.

Jose Maria shifted restlessly. "Is it of the child you wish to speak?" he blurted. "Have you learned its sex yet?"

His words died on the silent air that smelled of roots and charcoal and the sweat of suppliants. When the stationary figure spoke, it was in a voice as neuter as a statue's.

"How fares the foot, Jose Maria?"

"It is better, thanks." He smiled ingratiatingly. "It has begun to heal itself."

Now Tia Caridad swayed forward, her huge breasts laboring unevenly.

"And your *field*? Will it next begin to seed itself while you sow mischief with the foreigner?"

Startled at her intensity he stammered, "We do but dig a little in the ground. It is a pastime which diverts him, and he pays me well. Five pesos every day in silver."

"And you have dug for five days now in the dwelling

of the Old Ones. Do you know how much you will have earned tomorrow?"

"Thirty pesos, señora." And the day after, thirty-five, and the day beyond that, if it lasted—

"Thirty pesos of silver," she repeated. "And do you know, Jose Maria, how much the bones and body of Our Lord were sold for?" The woman's features churned like something undergoing fermentation. "Fool! What do you think the Desecrator digs for if it be not *bones*?"

And suddenly it made dread sense. With the sensation of a dark hand closing on his heart, Jose Maria could only whisper:

"But what can he seek to use them for?"

"That he may grow new flesh on them," she said, "and set them to walk again at his command."

"But this is impossible!"

Tia Caridad kept silent.

"Surely this cannot be possible, señora?"

She shrugged, like a hummock shifting in an earthquake. "Who knows? Did he not grow new flesh upon your foot?"

With unsteady hands, Jose Maria fumbled the day's five-peso piece from his pocket. "Help me," he said. "I can pay."

Tia Caridad drew back in alarm. "*His* silver? Would I not be damned as well as you?" And while he stared at her she went on relentlessly, "No, what is done is done. We can only hope the punishment will not be

suffered by the fruit your woman carries. Have you
dreamt no dreams of late?"

He shook his head numbly.

"None at all? Nor your woman?"

He hesitated. "There was a dream the woman had,
a few nights past. It was of no consequence. She merely
saw a bird in search of corn."

"A *bird*? And you can say this has no consequence,
Jose Maria? What creatures do you think the Old
Ones send as messengers—a jackass like yourself? Can
a jackass fly?"

His ignorance shamed him more than her contempt.

"Speak, man! I cannot save you if you lie. Did the
bird bring something in its beak?"

"I do not know, señora, truly! It was not my dream."

She slumped back in dismissal. "Go, then, and have
the woman probe her memory."

As Jose Maria started for the door, the brazier flared
up with a hiss. He turned to see Tia Caridad lowering
a pudgy hand to her lap. There was the scent of rosin
in the air.

"With luck," she said, "your son may still be spared."

In the new night, señor Bredi sat before a fire kindled
less for heat, it would appear, than company. His pipe
hung slackly from his jaw, his features loose with re-
verie. There were no tokens or omissions setting him
apart from natural men. Jose Maria continued watching him from the darkness, aware of the nearby field
he had abandoned for some child's game suddenly com-

posed of sinister forfeits. And aware, more violently, of wildly sweeter harvests; of the ripening in his woman's belly, named and contained now in its blurry male appendages, spark given shape. Once again exhilaration filled him, only to give way to dread. With all his senses whetted to acuteness, he stepped into the firelight.

"Jose! You surprised me."

As señor Bredi scrambled to his feet, could one glimpse shadow relapsing into flesh?

"What is it, man? Is something wrong?" he asked sharply.

"No, señor! Nothing!"

Señor Bredi examined him in curiosity. "Be seated, I will bring the flask."

"Please do not trouble yourself," Jose Maria said quickly. "I cannot remain. I am on my way to Confession," he lied, watching the other one closely.

But señor Bredi did no more than shrug. "What is it you wish, then?"

"Only to inform you, señor, that I can work for you no longer."

With a sigh, señor Bredi stooped to prod the fire. There was a look of disappointment on his face, but nothing more revealing. "Is it a question of the wages?"

Jose Maria shook his head, wondering how high this one was prepared to bid for him, but afraid to learn. "It is my season's crop. I will have none if I tarry."

"Yes, I suppose you are right. For myself I am sorry, but I wish you luck."

The easy victory caught him off balance. "I too am sorry. For this means your work will now be halted, *verdad?*"

"Oh no, there remains but little. I can finish by myself."

Jose Maria felt a convulsion of despair.

"Señor, believe me, there is nothing worth your labor here! Farther to the north—I will give you clear directions—you can dig for treasure," he stammered. "There you will find silver of a quantity to break your burro's back!"

As señor Bredi smiled, the firelight on his lenses made his eyes appear as empty sockets. "But it is not silver that I seek, Jose."

The woman did not hear him enter the hut. She was kneeling at the brazier, her eyes held by its embers. In the faint red light her bigness was continuous with shadow. Her head was cocked, as if the echo of activity still lingered on an inner ear. As Jose Maria came forward she glanced up with a vacant smile.

"It moved."

He squatted opposite her, watching to see if it would come again, life rippling across her abdomen like the Spirit passing on the waters of the deep.

She laughed in gentle condescension. "Now it sleeps. Do you want some *caldo?*" She began ladling chicken broth from the simmering pot into a cup.

"Later, perhaps." He had no appetite.

She passed him the cup. "The work is tiring. You must eat for strength."

"The work is finished."

"So soon?" His woman waited, but he decided he could tell her nothing.

Lowering his eyes to the cup, he sipped from it mechanically.

"Something troubles you," she said.

Jose Maria looked up gratefully. "I worry for the child. That you may fall and injure it, or that it might be marked in some way. Each day when I am gone so many things could happen." He emptied the cup back into the pot. "Tell me of your dream once more."

"My dream?" she smiled.

"The bird, the bird," he said impatiently.

"Ah, *that* dream."

"You have had others, then?"

"No. I do not think so." She frowned uncertainly. "Could this give the child a birthmark?"

"If it has, it is beyond repair. Let us consider graver things we might avert." He hesitated, then plunged ahead. "For example, was this bird you saw a female?"

"I don't remember. Why?"

"Don't argue, woman. *Think*. Have you never heard of birds that can give hatch to serpents?"

"Yes, of course."

"And could not such a bird deposit her egg for our hens to cover?"

His charged words echoed in the silent hut as both of them completed the picture in imagination. The woman stared at Jose Maria, hugging herself to still her trembling. He reached across the brazier, awkwardly gathering her shoulders in his hands. She began crying silently.

"No," he said, "calm yourself. Things cannot happen when we know how to meet them. This that I spoke of is not likely to pass. Just take heed when you collect the eggs."

She nodded vigorously.

"Collect them in the heat of midday. Better yet, leave them for me."

"Yes, maybe that is best."

"It is probably something else the bird intends. Was it a crow? If one splits a crow's tongue he can speak like a parrot. Tell me everything again, from the beginning . . ."

And though he questioned her at length on each detail, no matter how trivial, there was little she could add. The bird was big, black, and oppressive, but why she could not say. There was only the memory of those great searching circles it kept tracing.

It was past the hour of retirement when they left off, but sleep did not come easily to either of them. Sometime toward morning Jose Maria awoke, thinking that the woman had cried out. But she insisted it was nothing more than gas pains.

Shortly afterwards he drove the old ox to the field, resolving that the poor brute would know no rest until his plowing was completed. Señor Bredi finally emerged from his lean-to and called a sleepy greeting to him.

Then he held his head in suffering to pantomime a *cruda.* Seeing the hung-over Northerner going about his breakfast chores in the blunt light of day somewhat dispelled last night's anxieties. Jose Maria could even weigh the luxury of regret for having left him. Aside from the lavish wages, he had enjoyed the companionship and a certain sense of importance from their association. This, plus curiosity, caused him to climb the hill at day's end.

Peering down into the pit, he saw señor Bredi working at the bottom with a trowel. Beneath his feverish scraping a worn stone altar was being to emerge, hollowed in the center to receive who knew what kind of offering? And who knew what was buried at its base, or why this señor was so ravenous to reach it?

The woman's scream jerked him awake.

She lay wrenched in the serape, hugging her midriff and thrashing her head and shoulders like a flail. As she gathered herself to scream again, Jose Maria pulled her upright. Her eyes rolled open, white and unseeing. Then they focused and she collapsed against him, weeping in relief. It started her coughing.

"*Ay,*" she gasped, "*ay, corazón de Jesús!* If I had slept a moment longer . . ."

"It was the bird?"

She nodded, shuddering.

"And it was the bird last night that woke you."

"Yes, I could not speak of it. It *recognized* me," she said in awe. "*I* was what it had been searching for.

It was high, high up, but still it saw me. It folded its wings and began dropping toward me like a stone. And then I started running and woke up."

Jose Maria gentled her the way one would a panicked horse. "And tonight?" he said, for it could not be postponed.

"Tonight it found me. Just when I had reached my time. I was on my knees, about to give birth, and just as his little head began to issue from me—" she broke off, commencing to hiccough.

And now Jose Maria could no longer doubt the witch woman.

When his woman resumed, her voice was dazed with loathing. "I felt it settle on my shoulder. I couldn't turn my head. And then I saw its beak dip past me. It hung there, oh so long and sharp above my loins, waiting for the little eyes to—I thought somehow of grapes, the way a robin on a grapevine—"

"Enough!"

She blinked, reawakening to terror. "Is there nothing we can do?" she whispered.

"Yes, there is something," Jose Maria told her. "I will do it when the day comes. Now let us neither speak nor sleep till then."

As soon as there was light to see by, he made his way to señor Bredi's camp site. The burro staked nearby lifted its head in recognition. He had pulled a wild radish for it once. Now its idle days would end.

Inside the canvas lean-to, señor Bredi's digging tools lay beside the bag in which he slept. Jose Maria nudged him with his foot until he awoke, thick with surprise as he groped for his eyeglasses. Ignoring his questions, Jose Maria tossed the five days' wages on the ground.

"Take your silver, load your animal and leave," he said, in neither fear nor anger. "Your purpose cannot be accomplished here." He selected a spade from the heaped tools. "With your permission, I will borrow this."

Quickly climbing to the hilltop, he stood for a moment at the pit whose edges were piled with loose earth high as his waist. Then he leaned against the dirt wall, levering the spade in an attempt to create a landslide. A wild shout from below halted him. Señor Bredi was scrambling up the hill barefooted, his face stiff with outrage. He had almost reached the pit when Jose Maria called:

"Beware!" He swung the spade up, down, and sideways, tracing a formidable cross on the air between them. "You shall not blind my son to gain these bones."

"You superstitious fool, have you lost your senses? What is this you rave of?"

Nevertheless he remained fixed in place, Jose Maria noted in satisfaction. "These bones will never be disturbed," he repeated, turning back to complete his task of interment.

"Bones? Are you saying there are *bones* down there?"

And before he could protect himself the fiend was on him. Seized from behind, he felt the spade being wrested from him. He closed his eyes, lashing out in a fury of despair. The spade met something solid. Jose Maria gaped in surprise at the sight of señor Bredi reeling against the embankment, momentarily vulnerable. With his eyeglasses dangling from one ear as blood trickled down his cheek, he had the appearance of some palely huge, beached fish.

Sobbing in relief, Jose Maria leaped forward and drove the spade home again and again. . . .

When the rage passed, señor Bredi lay crumpled at his feet, smaller in death if he were truly dead. At least he wasn't breathing for the moment. Jose Maria waited till his limbs ceased trembling, and then before the strength entirely left them he wrestled the body onto the embankment. Sliding the spade beneath it, he pried it toppling into the pit. It lay face down on the eroded altar, the blood from its heavy gashes beginning to collect in the hollowed stone. The sight of these wounds, combined with his own light-headedness, gave Jose Maria a brief and sacrilegious vision of Our Lord. Had this Señor not washed Jose Maria's feet, and had He not cured the sick?

But afterwards, hauling the lean-to and all that it contained up the hill for burial, he realized that señor Bredi was merely a mortal vessel for Our Lord's dark twin, the Antichrist: charged, for sins too monstrous and ancient for conception, to wander foreign lands and epochs with a pouch of silver for the tempting of men's souls.

Jose Maria smiled, hefting the worn leather pouch to hear the jingling of corruption, Mexican pesos, North

American dollars, Roman, Arabian, Chinese who-knew-whats, all values to all men of wavering faith. Then he cast it down into the pit, to rot with all the rest of the effects. When he finished covering them, there were mounds of dirt left over. But eventually the elements would level them, if not this season then another.

Releasing the ass that had brought señor Bredi to the pueblo, he sent it on its way with a slap on the rump.

The midwife lingered in the doorway of the hut, her duties over. The knotted strings around the pallet had been cut to make birth easier, the blood was staunched, the cord tied cleanly. Again she voiced congratulations, and again Jose Maria smiled foolishly. When she was gone he squatted to watch his woman, overcome by sleep in the midst of nursing a healthy, though not really handsome son. The boy would be named for the Saint whose day this was. San Mateo, was it? A commonplace name. Peace, then, small Mateo, lest your holy namesake be insulted by another choice and withdraw his protection.

The woman had come partway awake, smiling up at him.

"I dreamed of the bird again," she murmured. "Do you remember?"

"Yes, I remember," he said. "But it cannot harm us any more."

"I know, because in my dream it flew away. Far

over the hills, so faaar . . ." And she herself was distant
once again in sleep.

The long vigil had kinked his muscles. Easing them,
Jose Maria stepped out into the morning streets to receive the compliments due him. He had expected to
be the sole topic of the day's discussion. But now he
saw that something else was competing with him for
attention.

A knot of restless villagers was gathering at the roadside. As he approached, a squat brown automobile
driven by two soldiers drew up, caked with the dirt of
its journey from the valley or from even farther. An
officer climbed out of the rear seat and slapped the
dust from his booted trousers. The soldiers, too, got
out and slouched in boredom beneath their rifles. There
was a seal on the side of the automobile, an eagle with
a snake seized in its beak. The snake, Jose Maria supposed, was the enemy of the Mexican government.

The officer commenced his questioning and the great
black bird continued flying, its beak red and replete
with the only thing it had been seeking, the patrimony
of Jose Maria's son.

FORWARDING SERVICE

*I*f pain hit when he was dozing, he would awaken instantly because it was the left side. And even though the pain was in the wrong location, all that his lulled mind could initially report was terror on the left. It was humiliating to be braced in a constant cringe. For years now, he had been creeping past obstacles of exertion. And scarcely into his forties he had developed an old man's gait and an old man's apprehensions.

Shifting position gingerly, Phillip lay there, conscious of his throbbing kidney and of the sounds and vistas of the six-bed ward as it sailed through another evening under banked riding lights. Smoke rose from the busted hip across the aisle as it lay monitoring an earphone, and other colleagues snored or muttered in response to footsteps of the uninfirmed, a separate race, as they pursued their unearned liberty down distant hallways. The night music would later be augmented by an ambulance soloing its arrival or the muffled harmonies of bedpans being washed. And after three evenings of it Phillip was almost glad that the decision for surgery had been made. (He pictured it as something like cleaning out a carburetor. How did a man get gravel in his kidney in the first place?)

Meanwhile, his heart continued prowling his chest like the caged, manic animal it was. A vicious brute requiring twenty-four-hour humoring, it could leap free the first time you got distracted by a little binge, or even pulled too tightly on a shoelace—and strike both you and itself a mortal wound. And whenever it did, would there be anyone to care? He tried to tell himself that he had made it through other lonely midnights, and he would get through this one, somehow. He could do it, if he had to.

Time passed, as it had to. And finally, with relief, he heard the tread of Herb, the night attendant. His figure bulked up in the half-light as he set the tray down on the bed table.

"How'd it go this evening, Mr. DeWitt?"

"Not too badly, thanks," Phillip said.

Herb switched on the bed lamp, his craggy, compassionate features searching Phillip's. He was a large man with a gentle touch.

"This should let you get a little sleep." As he prepared the syringe, he said, "Which arm'll it be?"

"Doesn't matter."

Phillip felt the cool swab of alcohol, the needle's sting, then settled back while Herb pulled up a chair to have a smoke. He, too, was single, Phillip had discovered; somewhere in his middle fifties, with a good portion of them spent right here. Not the most significant career one might elect, but for a man unburdened by either ambition or special skills, set in his easygoing ways, it was probably a comfortable enough existence. In addition, he ran a business on the side that, from all Phillip could gather about it, sounded more like a hobby than a source of revenue.

"Well, all set for tomorrow morning?" Herb asked.

Phillip smiled. "Suppose I could ask for a rain check?"

Herb chuckled.

"Seriously though, I'm a little worried, Herb. I have a fairly weak heart."

"I know. I saw your cardiogram."

Phillip waited.

"Well, what do you think?" he asked at last.

After a moment Herb said, "At least you'll have a good anesthetist in Dr. Abrahms."

But it came too late to be entirely reassuring. And at this stage Phillip wasn't particularly interested in any honest answers.

At last, Herb broke the intolerable pause to ask,

"Remember the girl I was telling you about just the other night, Mr. DeWitt?"

"What? Oh yes, Milly."

"Myra. M-Y-R-A," Herb said, in soft reproach. "Of course, she isn't a girl any longer because it happened quite a while back. Anyway, do you remember the man involved?"

"Afraid not."

"Ackerman. Paul Ackerman."

"That's right, I got it now. Myra and Paul Ackerman."

Phillip's gratitude for a little conversation before the sedative took hold was undercut by his annoyance at Herb's capacity for wandering. Like all bad story-tellers, he got mired in petty details and forgot the meat of the anecdote.

"And Myra was one of your clients," Phillip said, remembering. "What was it this Ackerman fellow did to her, anyway?"

"It must have been something terrible. She never would tell me."

"Dear God," Phillip thought with a tired smile. But the drowsiness was setting in, and any kind of talk was an improvement over silently listening to his own heart. Poor Myra, and poor Ackerman, whose garbled histories were lost in Herb's diffusiveness. However it was that Ackerman had hurt her, Myra had a change of feeling years later and wanted to let him know he could come home; all was forgiven.

"Come home, all is forgiven," Phillip murmured.

"You must get some pretty weird clients, Herb. But then, that service you run sounds pretty much on the weird side, too."

Herb chuckled, but only after an instant's hesitation in which Phillip realized he had been hurt.

"I mean, it's a little out of the ordinary line of messenger services, you'll have to admit."

"Oh, no doubt about it, Mr. DeWitt. But it fills a real need. You see, when someone you have a violent emotion about disappears without a trace, it can be pretty frustrating if you can't get word to them. I'd like to think that I take over at the point where the Dead Letter Office quits."

"I suppose the missing persons bureau wouldn't be available for your clients," Phillip said, as numbness nibbled at his outer fringes, "since the people they're trying to get in touch with haven't broken any laws."

"Well, I don't know about that," Herb said. "I mean, whether or not you have to be involved in crime before the missing persons bureau will step in. But in any case, it's always too late to call in any authorities."

"What do you do, then? Run advertisements?"

"Well, not exactly. It's a sort of word-of-mouth arrangement." And even with his eyes closed, Phillip could sense Herb's awkwardness. "I just try to pass the information on, to whoever's liable to be in contact."

Phillip laughed sleepily. "My God, Herb, do you make any kind of income with such a sloppy system?"

And again he realized by the silence that he had hurt the older man. "I'm sorry, Herb, it's just that—"

"It's all right, Mr. DeWitt. I haven't been explaining it well, but it isn't easy to explain. There's no income involved," Herb said quietly. "I wouldn't capitalize on people's feelings. Besides, I can't even be positive that messages always get delivered. I do a certain amount of duplication, of course. Still, that's all my clients have to go on. . . ."

Phillip felt he must have missed something. And while he descended like a stone toward slumber, ripples of consciousness receding from him, he wondered if he should become a client of Herb's. Was there anyone whom he had had a violent emotion about who could be told, "Come home, all is forgiven?" There may have been, but violent emotions were all in Phillip's past. With a heart like his, they were too costly a luxury.

Dimly, he heard Herb saying, "You awake, Mr. De-Witt?"

Phillip opened his eyes, turning to Herb with a smile. And now he remembered his question. "I don't understand about your messengers, Herb. What kind of people are they?"

"They're just ordinary, nice folks like yourself, Mr. DeWitt."

Curiosity made Phillip more awake. "But where do you get them, and what do you—"

"Why, I find them right here on the graveyard shift," Herb said as gently as he could.

Fully alert now, Phillip sat upright and stared at him.

"By the way, Mr. DeWitt," he said, "on that message to Paul Ackerman from Myra? It's not 'Come home, all is forgiven.' It's just 'All is forgiven.'"

Phillip began trembling.

"And one more, if it's all right with you," Herb continued. "It's to Stanley Papadakis: P-A-P-A-, like in papa; D-A-K-I-S."

"Get out of here," Phillip said hoarsely. "You're a maniac!"

"No, I'm not." Herb rose reluctantly. "But I'm sorry you're taking it this way. I'm not responsible for the facts of life or death, Mr. DeWitt."

After a moment, Phillip said, "No, I guess you're not. What's the message to Papadakis?"

"That's better. I knew you were a gentleman, Mr. DeWitt."

"What's the message?"

"'We all miss you so.'" Herb hesitated, then said, "I guess I'll shove along now. No hurry on those, Mr. DeWitt. If you can't get to them just yet, they'll keep."

And listening to Herb's heavy tread going off, Phillip lay and wept the messages into his pillow, fixing them in his memory, knowing there was no one who would ever have to bring remembrances to him.

A WINTER'S
TALE

After the long, plum-heavy summer rains that had
quickened the angular corn patch and had brought the
calabashes to their meaty fulness, and after the gluts
of autumn dwindled, with the avocados coming scanty
and the old sow foraging among the lessening husks,
December had arrived again. Wind pushed its way up
the mountain, carrying a chill from the distant lake, but
the daubed wattles of the hut were sealed against it,
and the brazier burned in bright defiance. Across its
glow, the old woman covertly studied the face of her
great-grandson.

Masked by shadow, the frail, five-year-old features

seemed to alter, as if the old woman, in a momentary gift of second sight, had glimpsed the male-to-be: a grinning city lout drunkenly whooping his horse down his fiancée's street and firing his pistol to impress her with his manhood; and for feed for his horse, bullets for his pistol, liquor for his zest, and the fiesta for his bride, he would undergo a constant, frenzied pursuit of pesos. But now, stuffed with the supper that the land yielded freely or the neighbors bartered, innocent of itches, the boy played in contentment with the thing that would one day lure him from her. It was a silver peso given him yesterday by his Uncle Nacho, her shiftless grandson who had climbed the mountain for the anniversary of the burial of his sister, the boy's mother. She had died last year of the fits, four years after returning from Jocotepec to give birth to a father-less child.

"What shall I buy with my peso, *abuelita*?" the boy finally asked.

It was the question she had been anticipating all day.

"Buy?" the old woman said dubiously. "Let me see it." She hefted the coin with the engraving of a vulture attempting a devour a snake, ran an arthritic finger over the lettering that neither of them could read. Then she raised it up to her mouth. "Is it savory to eat?"

"No," the boy giggled.

"Ah, then it is a seed of some kind. If you plant it in the ground, it will grow."

"No, it won't!"

"No? Then it must be that you can cook in it. Has your peso the capacity to hold a chicken stew?"

"No!" the boy laughed explosively.

"Then it is worth nothing in this village." She threw it back to him in contempt. "People are not crazy here. To exchange your peso, you must go to the city where the crazy ones live, like your Uncle Nacho."

The words were harsher than she had intended, but the old woman had been racked with jealousy all day before at the sight of the boy eagerly trailing after Nacho and ingesting his lies like a famished weasel at a pullet's throat.

The boy looked as if he had been slapped. His mouth, still wide from laughter, began quivering. "I shall!" he cried. "I shall buy what I want in the city with my peso, and when it is all spent I shall live with Uncle Nacho."

"Go, then. And see if the city wastes you into nothing as it did your mother."

"I don't care! I shall leave tomorrow."

Gripping the peso in his fist, as if defying her to pry it from him, he rolled over on his stomach. The old woman watched him from the isolation of her separate hurt, picturing him working down the mountain below which Lake Chapala began its vast spread in the tumbling distances. On its shores were cities with hundreds of inhabitants in each, and at the other end spawled Chapala itself, its broad, cobbled streets lined with handsome houses of adobe and now and then the carriages that she remembered from her girlhood (all replaced by machines, if rogues like Nacho could be believed)—a numberless swarm of vendors selling the superfluities of life to one another by a system of hours of laboring for others than oneself. And somewhere beyond Chapala lay even grander cities, till one reached the very capital of Mexico, which could swallow ten Chapalas and not even feel a bellyache. And still beyond, across an ocean in which ten Lake Chapalas would be lost, lay entire other countries: Spain, China, and that of the English, a land of Protestant millionaires where no one ever had to labor. . . . Ay, it was a huge and growing world, and the total anonymity of it frightened her. But to a young boy, secure in his vitality and ignorance, no doubt it represented opportunity.

He wouldn't leave tomorrow, of course, but in the ruins of the church his future could be read as in the dregs of a teacup. It had been years since the village could support a priest, the people had diminished so. Priests used to visit every year or so, to perform marriages and administer other sacraments, but now there were too few young people left to be worth a padre's efforts. The last one had trekked in when Nacho and his sister had been baptized (the older grandchildren had by then departed), and it was evident that there would be no others.

Suddenly the old woman had a vision of herself abandoned, her last pigling traded off, her sow dead or running wild in the lowlands, her corn patch choked by vines, and herself, in a living graveyard, too weak to find her way down to the lakeshore. It was a vision of such clarity that she knew it was her destiny. With a mixture of fear and cunning, she kneeled beside the sprawling boy. Face streaked with dried tears, he had fallen asleep in exhaustion from the intensity of his emotions. Such a fragile crutch to lean on, she thought, but it is all I have.

She began humming a brisk ranchero song, and when his eyelids fluttered she knew he was awake.

"Would you like to hear how one man fared in the city?" she murmured. "It will give you other thoughts about the pleasures of the city life."

He kept his eyes closed to punish her, but of course he was listening intently. Returning to her chair, she tried to sort out the events as she recalled them. She had difficulty remembering things in recent years, and this that she wished to relate had all happened in her own great-grandmother's day, or even earlier.

"Many years ago," she began, "in a village far from here, there lived a wise, kind man. He never got drunk, never got into fights, and was said to have the ability to heal numerous ailments in both animals and people. If he had remained in his village," she said, "he could have lived out his years in peace and honor. But instead, he went one day to the city." Just why he did, the old woman couldn't remember, if she'd ever known. "It was a long burro ride away, and when he arrived it was midday, and time for the meal. Consequently, he seated himself in the shade of a mango tree, and

just as he unwrapped his pork tacos, the Evil One rode
up to him on a horse."

The old woman was pleased to see the boy's cheek
twitch.

"For, as the whole world knows, the Evil One is
found only in cities," she lied. "Then the Evil One
spoke: 'Señor, never have I seen tacos as appetizing
as those. I will trade you my pistol for one. It is a
pistol which never runs out of bullets, no matter how
often it is fired.' And he produced a magnificent pistol
with a pearl handle and butt of beaten gold, which,
as he had promised, was a magic pistol. And do you
know what the wise man told him?"

The old woman waited while the boy's fists clenched.

"He said, 'Many thanks for your offer, señor, but a
pistol would be of no use to me. There is no man I
call enemy.' Thus the wise man survived the first
temptation. Then the Evil One spoke again: 'Señor, I
cannot leave till I have tasted of those tacos. Here,
take my horse for one. It is a horse which never re-
quires feed, no matter how hard you work him.'" And
the old woman began describing the horse to the boy,
inventing a horse of all horses which could run like
the wind and never tire. "Again, the wise man spoke:
'To my profound regret, señor, I must decline your
offer, for I prefer to ride by burro.'"

The boy couldn't stand it any longer. He jumped
up and ran to the old woman's side. "But why, *abuelita*,
why? Was he a crazy one?"

"No, of course he was not a crazy one," she said irritably. "He was a wise man, and he knew with whom he was treating. If you traffic with the Evil One, you are doomed for eternity." She noted in satisfaction how the boy's eyes widened. "That was the second temptation," she said. "Then for the third time the Evil One spoke: 'Señor, the smell of those tacos is maddening. Take my purse for one. It is a purse which always contains one silver peso, no matter how often you remove it.' And at this the wise man said, 'Silver betrays.' And he crossed himself, and the Evil One disappeared in a puff of smoke."

The boy was silent in wonder. While he was still thronging with questions, the old woman said, "And fix yourself on this—that wise man was right. He had the power of prophecy, for silver sent him to his death. Shall I tell you how he died?"

The boy nodded in eager apprehension and she leaned forward, prepared to inflict the moral of her story in all its terrible immensity. Then at the sight of his waiting eyes, so open and vulnerable, she relented. How could one describe such a happening like that to a child?

"Sit yourself," she said, and when he had climbed into her lap she rocked his head against her breast. "It was a hard, undeserved death. Few men have had a worse one. The people who beset him were cultureless barbarians. You will hear of it when you are older."

For if love cannot bind him to me, she thought, how can terror?

"What was his name, *abuelita*?"

"The same as yours," she said.

"Jesús Gomez Ordoño?" the boy exclaimed in awe.

"No, no. Jesús Cristo."

"Cristo," the boy repeated uncertainly. "Jesús Cristo what? What was his mother's family?"

"Don't fret yourself," the old woman told him. "It was a decent, respectable family."

The boy yawned. "Against all that, I think he was a fool," he said sleepily. "I would have taken the horse."

He can say such things in purity, she thought, because he is yet unbaptized. But perhaps he is right, scandalous as it sounds. For if they could put an honest man like that to such a death, what chance did lesser men have? Though of course the purse, not the horse, was the correct choice, because if there was anything that city people hated more than honesty, it was poverty.

BEACHHEAD
IN BOHEMIA

*H*erbert Whipple slowed to an uncertain halt in front of the apartment house. The number was plain enough, even through the narrowing dusk; and on reexamination, it still checked with the address in his briefcase. Eight hundred and fifty North Montgomery was a paint-worn frame building with a weary posture and an incompleted look, whose knuckled street door stood equally open to the weather and to random visitors. It lifted wobbly above a shallow street that seemed composed of art supply shops and weakly lit bars. Herbert entered, feeling his way along the darkened hall and up a railless flight of stairs. As he passed the second floor landing, he could hear a distant babble of voices, and occasionally the sound of a table being thrown across the room, together with its dishes. Encouraged by this evidence of life he climbed to the top floor, and finding a door at the rear with a wedge of light beneath it, knocked. There was a muffled shout of invitation. He stepped inside, then started to back out in embarrassment. A couple were seated at a table in the center of the bare, box-shaped room.

The woman was blonde, with sleepy features and a dynamically proportioned body. She was completely nude. Beside her, a large bearded man, heavily dressed against the draft, was cutting slices of salami and cramming them (along with equal quantities of beard) into his mouth. He waved with his free hand, making the same unintelligible noises of welcome. Herbert came forward uneasily. He found himself noticing that the blonde's legs were lightly goose-pimpled, and hastily glanced aside. There was an easel in the corner, with a painting of what might have been the woman at the table, being also a blonde. But the girl on the easel had several heads, and was flat and triangular in locations where the model was noticeably not. He watched the bigger man lean back from the table, wiping his beard with a handkerchief. Standing there in his old but neatly pressed gray suit—a slightly round shouldered man of average looks, tastes, and fears (and happy with them), not particularly needing a shave or a haircut—Herbert felt strangely formal and conspicuous.

"Good evening." He cleared his throat. "I'm from

Ide and Whipple, Income Tax Consultants. I'm trying
to locate a—"

"Income Tax!" the big man shouted. "For what,
Income Tax!" He lurched to his feet and Herbert
quickly stepped back. But the man was smiling hugely
through his beard. He emptied the contents of his
pockets on the table and flung out his arm. "That's
how much Income Tax! Take it, go on!"

Herbert blinked at the scanty pile of coins, streetcar
transfers and bitten pencils. "I'm afraid there's some
misunderstanding—"

But the artist had turned back to the blonde, speaking to her between explosions of laughter. "This fellow
wants Income Tax—do you hear, Katya?" he shouted.
"I gave him from my pockets and told him, take it!
There's your Income Tax!"

Herbert tried again to get in a word of protest. "It's
all a mistake, if you'd only—"

"Come, I show you my Income." Clamping Herbert's
arm, the big man led him over to the easel. "With
your own eyes, look!" He pointed. "Is this a *Saturday
Evening Post* cover, I should get five thousand dollars
Income?"

"No," Herbert said apprehensively, "I'll have to
admit—"

But again the artist turned to translate for his model.
"Katya, my plum!" he yelled happily. "This fellow
thinks it's a *Saturday Evening Post* cover, ten thousand
dollars Income he could Tax me!"

However, Katya still didn't seem to hear—although

his voice surely carried to the lower floors. Herbert stared down at the floor, defeated. He began to feel the stirrings of hunger. He had come directly here from the office, without stopping at home for dinner. He glanced up, and his gaze wandered wistfully between the salami leavings on the table and the nude, indifferent blonde.

"I guess I got it wrong," he sighed. "It must be South Montgomery that my client—"

"Of course, South Montgomery Street!" the artist bellowed agreeably. "That's where the bloodsuckers live, the millionaire critics! You want Income Tax, that's where you'll go look—"

"Yes, well, perhaps you're right," Herbert said quickly. "Thanks, anyway . . ."

He backed from the room, pulling the door shut. Inside, he could hear Katya being told exactly what had happened.

It was too late to take a bus to the other end of town. He didn't feel like going home. But then he seldom felt like going home (except when his wife was away), and he was hungry, so he started for home. Descending the stairs, he thought about Katya, and of what his wife would say if he asked her to sit at the table with her clothes off. And worse, if she would do it. Down on the second floor, he found that the party had grown larger and noisier, overflowing into the hall. The guests seemed oddly suspicious of one another. They milled in separate groups, drinks in hand, beyond a door that stood open on a congested, foggy apartment. As he began cautiously pushing through them, a tall, bony woman with pimples caught his arm.

"Tell us what *you* think, she yelled angrily. "Do singing commercials use masochistic symbolism?"

"Well, I never really followed them . . ." Herbert stammered.

"There, you see?" she said to someone else, and shoved him away.

He was given a push from another direction, and gradually he found himself being elbowed farther into the crowd.

"Please, I have to go home," he called.

A sallow-faced man turned. "But one can't go home, you know," he said. "I mean, not really. The womb has been rented."

And then the press of people carried him forward like a tide, depositing him inside the doorway of the apartment. Herbert stood there, collecting himself as he stared around the tall, deep room. It was difficult to see in its entirety, through the kelp-thick smoke. But it had clashing, print-hung walls, and seemed made up of completely random furniture, with numerous little halls and alcoves that apparently led to other rooms. Just then, a soft-eyed little man in a maroon sport shirt hurried over to him. He spoke while looking slightly to the side, as if he had astigmatism.

"You haven't a drink," he said. "*You're* antisocial."

"I'm not much of a drinker," Herbert said. "I can't handle it too well."

"That's all right, I'm antisocial, too," the little man

said. "But there's utterly no alcohol in *these* drinks." He took Herbert's arm. "Have just one, do."

"Well, if that's the case . . ." Herbert let himself be led over to a corner table that held a large punch bowl. He sampled a Dixie cup full of something that tasted like a mixture of hair tonic and lemonade, but felt pleasantly warming. He smiled his appreciation at the little man, who had forgotten to let go his arm. "Not bad punch," he said, "I mean, for punch."

"Oh, yes, it's delicious," the little man said absently. He fingered Herbert's tie. "Do wear red all the time. It brings out your complexion."

"Why, thanks," Herbert said. "It's just something my wife picked up."

The little man nodded sadly. "I was afraid it was. Excuse me," he said, and hurried off.

Herbert watched him seek out another of the guests, apparently an old friend, since they disappeared into a corner to chat. Nice guy, he thought. He felt he really should leave, but it was so pleasant here compared to being home. The punch tasted better with each cupful (perhaps because he was hungry), and in a way it was as warm and refreshing as coffee. Presently the smoke made him feel a little giddy. He loosened his collar and, since other people were doing it, sat down on the floor. He listened for awhile to a couple conversing nearby. Something about Li'l Abner's Oedipus complex, but since he had missed the last few installments, he didn't feel qualified to join them. Instead, he watched a large, loose-moving colored man clacking a pair of spoons together for a solemn listener. It made a nice rhythm.

"You share the guilt," the listener told him angrily. "You're just as responsible for white chauvinism."

The colored man winked at Herbert, and Herbert grinned back. He felt pretty good, better than he had in months. Soon everyone was seated on the floor; then gradually, as if it were being slowly submerged, the room filled with quiet. If they were starting a game, it would be better to leave now. He had climbed part way to his feet when someone behind yanked him back into a sitting position. There, inertia took over. Oh well, he could always leave at the end of the game. The lights were turned down, and Herbert saw a plump man with a foot-long ebony cigarette holder rise to address the group. He had bad teeth, even in the uncertain light.

"To those literary few who have followed poetry in its emancipation, through Dada, the Surreal, Oral Expressionism and Anal Containment, and finally to Free-Associationism," the bulky man announced, "it can come as no surprise to learn that the ultimate form of communication must be nonwritten, or cerebral verse. For where the reflective mind intervenes, surely the poet is handcuffed to his pen." He coughed delicately. "We are privileged to have with us tonight an artist with whom cultured auditors are not unfamiliar— Villon . . ." he smiled, waiting for the stir of excitement to ease, "who will give a recital in Unpremeditated

Poetry." Villon rose from his chair and came forward, nodding irritably at the spatter of applause. He was a gaunt man with a face like an old gnome, wearing thick shell glasses and loose-hanging clothes. His heavy black hair grew straight up, like the bristles in a brush. He faced them with his hands jammed in his pockets.

"Goose!" he said. "Moose! Caboose!" Then Villon threw back his head and squinted up at the ceiling, as if searching for leaks.

"The train that runs 'tween uterus and hell," he intoned,

"Is twice as private as a padded cell."

He quickly raised his hand to halt the applause. Then, with his face puckering in concentration, he said: "Cell! Smell! Bell . . .

The churchbells weep, for I have just shot God:

He tried to come between me and my broad."

Herbert began giggling. He felt as relaxed and buoyant as a child at a birthday party. Gradually he became aware of silence, and realized that everyone had turned to stare at him. And now the fat man was pointing at him angrily and Villon was saying: "Very well, I relinquish the floor to you."

"Oh, is it my turn already?" Herbert said.

Several people pulled him to his feet (being unnecessarily rough about it, he thought). He walked across the tilting floor and turned to face them with a good-natured grin. Apparently it worked something like when grandma would get high on cough syrup and tell him nursery rhymes, getting them all mixed up.

That seemed roughly the idea, although he hadn't followed the rules too closely.

"Well, lemme see," he said, scratching his head. "Okay, here goes:
There was an old woman who lived in a hoop
Having too many children, she used them for soup.
Hey diddle diddle, the cat's turned brittle,
Little Jackie Horner, run for the coroner . . ."

It was fun. He closed his eyes and concentrated on not thinking of the words:
"Little boy blue, let fly your doves
The tree surgeon's pawned his rubber gloves.
The cow's in the pulpit, the clock is with child—
The hangman will come when his number's dialed."

There was a moment of stunned silence. Herbert cautiously opened his eyes. Then the applause hit him like a solid wall. He stood there, pleased and a little bewildered at the violence of their enthusiasm. People were coming up to pump his hand and heap him with questions:

"Do you work on other forms besides dactyl?"

"Is your use of assonance deliberate?"

"Am I right in detecting a Pound influence?"

"Maybe you're right . . . I'm not sure . . . I don't remember," was all he could say.

He had won the game, apparently. It was the first time he had ever won anything in his life. Suddenly he was surprised to feel someone take his arm and pull him through the crowd into a relatively quiet, shadowed corner. It was a woman, a compact blonde of

middle height, with an apple-smooth complexion and
deliberate eyes.

Possibly the model from upstairs, since it was so
easy, in fact inescapable, to picture her without any
clothes.

"You looked a little surrounded," she said. "I thought
you could use some air."

"Thanks, it's a fine idea," he said. "Are you the
hostess?"

"The hostess?" she said, puzzled. "Why, no."

"Well, who is? I mean, whose place is this?"

"I never thought about it. I'll see if I can find out."
She stepped close and squeezed his arm. "You're going
to do great things," she said. "*Great* things. And I'll
help you. You wait here."

Herbert watched her walk off, her hips swinging
high and tightly in her dimple-length skirt. No one
had ever talked to him that nicely, or looked at him
that way—especially since his marriage. But it was
getting more and more difficult to remember being
married. Suddenly he could hear Villon and the fat
man talking, just within earshot of him.

". . . stereotyped imagery he uses. I mean, really,"
Villon was saying bitterly. "And that transparent
Freudian symbolism. It's so obviously derivative of
Crane."

"Still, you have to give him credit for that Mother
Goose associational structure," the fat man said. "It
is pretty connotative."

"Yes, but such a cheap theatrical device . . ."

They walked off. Herbert wondered what they were arguing about. Just then there was a mild commotion near the doorway, and a newcomer pushed into the room. Without even removing his hat and topcoat, he tossed a magazine down on a table in the center. He spread it open and stood waiting until the room quieted.

"This happens to be the latest issue of the *Companionate Woman's Journal,*" he said in angry triumph. "I want all of you to see a poem here, written by a certain George Ketzel." People began turning toward Villon. "I think some of us know who Mr. Ketzel is."

Villon, or Ketzel, tried to smile, but couldn't make it. He took out a handkerchief and began blotting his neck.

"Tell us, Villon—" the man called, "how many pieces of silver did you get for this poem?"

An ugly murmur began circulating in the room.

"It was a joke," Villon said desperately. "I was boring from within . . ." He turned to the fat man, who had already begun walking away. "Jacques, you believe me, don't you? It was just a joke . . ."

The crowd closed in on him, shouting him down. There was something pitiful about it, even though Herbert didn't understand why they had suddenly turned on him. But he didn't get to see the rest, because by then the blonde had returned and was leading him away.

"Nobody seems to know who owns the apartment," she said.

"That's all right," he said. "Say, what's the fuss over there?"

"Disgusting, isn't it? That hack!" She hurried him through an alcove and into a small room, closing the door behind them. "We can talk here. Sit down, while I get comfortable."

There was no place to sit except the bed. Herbert perched on the edge of it, trying unsuccessfully not to watch the blonde through the porous curtains of what seemed to be a closet. She reappeared in a leaf-green hostess gown and seated herself beside him.

"You're so tense," she said, taking his hand. "Why don't you relax a little?"

They were just relaxing a little, when the door banged open. Villon stalked into the room. Herbert nervously watched him paw through the bureau, although the blonde took no notice. He soon left, with a small bundle of clothing under his arm. They got relaxed all over again.

"I'm Gretel," she said, presently.

"I'm Herbert," Herbert said, although introductions seemed a little beside the point at this stage.

Suddenly Villon charged into the room again, grabbed up a toothbrush and exited, slamming the door behind him. But by then, Herbert had become so acclimated to the environment that it didn't even constitute an interruption.

DARKLING
I LISTEN

In his dream, a Jimmy Lunceford record is coming from the spare receiver as he takes over. He types his sign in the log below the final entry of the man whom he relieves. His sign consists of the first and last letters of his name, or in the G.I. alphabet, Able Dog. It has a certain verve, he feels. He is happier being Able Dog than being Buck Sergeant Arnold, USAAF, 39535733.

The Lunceford recording (in his dream) throbs softly in the warm moist air of the quonset hut, like a vein in a dengue patient's temple. Outside, the sea swings quietly beneath a bomber's moon. Arnold isn't sched-

uled for this shift. He has traded with another trick
chief named Ben Levine (Love Easy). This is the time
of month when all the winnings from the smaller poker
games have gravitated to the Seabee Chiefs' game, and
Ben is kibitzing. But Arnold likes to work the mid-
watch. He has a beer left over from his weekly ration,
a tax-free cigar, and time to catch up on his corre-
spondence. It's a good white-collar job, as wars go; a
nice wet-collar job, if he pretends it's summer in Los
Angeles.

Down the row, Farniff, or Double Fox, or Fearless
Freddie, is simultaneously monitoring the Funafuti
circuit and last week's *Honolulu Advertiser*. And at
the far end of the bank of receivers, Cady, the new re-
placement, is intent upon the harmless chore that Ben
created for him. Every hour he answers the field phone
from Weather, copies the coded groups and earnestly
taps them out on the hand key. Then he logs this
achievement under his name, Cady. He is allowed no
sign. There is a Charlie Yoke on Johnson Island, a man
named Cassidy, whose reputation Sergeants Arnold
and Levine are protecting. Between weather broad-
casts Cady waits (helmet, carbine, bayonet within
reach) for the Japanese invasion.

Now Arnold eavesdrops on an aircraft frequency
named Topaz, by day a busy pond of air in the eight
thousand kilocycle band. His earphones, mineral sea
shells, chirp and sputter with the echo of those elec-
tronic depths. Canton Island tests his transmitter,
Hickam Field tests his: both clear as a bell here, over

the nice skip distances that prevail at night. Arnold
recognizes both operators by their fists. In the needless
exchange of signal strengths, they communicate pro-
hibited personal messages. It is accomplished through
a melange of formal international signals, obsolete
American telegraphy, ham language and hieroglyphs
that change almost nightly, in the ceaseless contest between the Army Airways Communication System and
its chaperone, the Army Signal Corps, recording everything. Any proven breach of radio security is a court-
martial offense.

Arnold joins them in a threesome. *Dit dit.*

Dit-dah-dah dit dit, Hickam asks (in that banana-
boat swing of his), a continent's length away. Who
dat?

Able Dog (preceded, of course, by the letter Q,
which makes it a legitimate Q signal, however irrele-
vant to this context).

Hey, old man, fine business, and the colloquy begins.
Has Arnold been in any good air raids lately? Not yet,
he tells them, hoping the curtness will convey a grim-
lipped hint of action to come. They conceal their envy
and assure him that their hearts bleed for him, that
the beer is cold and abundant where they are. Next,
they ask about the native women and again Arnold
strikes the expected posture, which he will maintain
at the NCO Club when he goes back to Oahu on ro-
tation: They're not bad, I'm doing all right. At least
they beat the girls on River Street . . . Regards to
everyone, 73's all around.

Arnold notes in the log that at 2400 the network is quiet, readability good.

Somewhere a speed key snickers. *Dah, dit, dit. Dit-dit-dit-dit dit dit.* Tee hee.

Someone yawns in answer: a drawn-out comma symbol, almost onomatopoetic. Wasn't there a guy on Fiji who used to send fraction bars whenever he was pissed-off?

Suddenly Arnold finds the idea of stylized emotions grotesque. He wonders if he would have made a good tail gunner. The bulk of his class at radio operators' school went on to gunnery school, where they graduated as Staff Sergeants. When Arnold saw them off they congratulated him on his less than 20-20 vision. He congratulated them on their rank-to-be: "A staff today, a stiff tomorrow." They all grinned feebly, remembering the sole advantage of a ground-bound radio op.: he is guaranteed survival. Arnold doesn't knock survival, but he feels that monotony is a high price to pay for it.

The Lunceford recording has been followed by Larry Clinton's "Deep Purple" as a nostaligic clincher. Now it's time for enlightenment. In bland British intonations, the announcer describes the toll of American ships and aircraft that the Japanese Imperial Forces have taken for the day, and the lively prospects for tomorrow.

Cady is indignant. "What's that, Tokyo Rose?"

"A prejudiced mind is a closed mind," Farniff says reprovingly. "We're getting the lowdown that the

AFRS doesn't dare put out. Oh well, we'll *win*. I
mean, in the long run. Yessir, the Golden Gate by
Fifty-eight—"

Just then they are told to stand by for a message to
an advance air base in the Central Pacific. They fall
silent.

"You men on Rocky Base, I am sorry to report, will
not live to see another full moon."

As they hear the code name of their own island,
Arnold and Farniff look at one another, remember to
smile. Cady's sullenness only deepens.

"This is one more regrettable consequence of your
government's insistence on meddling in the Pan Asiatic
Co-Prosperity Sphere. After all," the voice says reasonably, "shouldn't it be Asia for the Asians? Do we Asians
question the soundness of your Monroe Doctrine?
Same principle, isn't it?" A voice convincingly secure
of itself. Then it sighs. "Well, many other Americans
will have to die in foreign waters before your government accepts the inevitable. Meanwhile, what is it
like this very moment in your home town? Is it skating
weather? Is there ice on the pond and a bonfire on the
banks with weenies roasting . . . ?"

The voice blends into the theme song, Benny Goodman's "Down South Camp Meeting."

Stammering a little in his anger, Cady says, "I
thought this was a secret air base."

Farniff shrugs. "So now we're an unsinkable aircraft
carrier instead." He recovers some of his jauntiness.
"Don't worry, Cady, no matter how much stuff they

drop on us, this rock won't sink. The taxpayers' investment is safe." He turns to Arnold, gestures inclusively. "How much you figure all this is costing?"

"All of it?" Arnold can't even begin to guess. The detachment of Seabees who built and maintain the airstrip; the marine anti-aircraft battalion who theoretically defend it; all the Army, Navy and Air Force housekeepers and bookkeepers like himself; and finally —what's it all about—the two squadrons of B24's, their crews, mechanics and armorers, who are starting to soften up their next-door neighbor for what may be an invasion attempt or merely a feint. "Millions," he says. "At least."

"And suppose they take this frigging—what's its name?"

"Tarawa."

"OK, Tarawa. Suppose they take it? What then?"

Arnold shakes his head. "A lot of islands between here and Japan."

"A hell of a lot of islands," Farniff nods. "Maybe I better put some pressure on my congressman. See if I can't get home in time for the weenie roast."

But before Arnold can ask him how he plans to get it past the censor, that wonderfully husky voice comes on. Arnold turns up the volume and the quonset fills with warmth and tolerance.

"Hello, fellows. How are all my boy friends?" She has a sly guilty laugh, as if apologizing for the news that has preceded her. She sounds as if she's just made love, or is just about to, and doesn't give a damn for any other occupation now. Arnold pictures her as a girl without a country, perhaps some UCLA co-ed visiting her parents' homeland at Pearl Harbor, and trapped into doing this.

"This is your old girl friend again, Little Orphan Annie," she says. "Well, I got mine today. Japanese soldier got his today. I imagine your girl is getting hers. You getting yours?" She puts another record on while we think about it.

"God *damn*," Farniff says appreciatively. "Listen, you suppose Levine is getting any push-push off these gooks?"

"If he is, he's the only guy here." The native women are mostly fat and prudish, with a marinated odor.

"He must be half gook himself the way he sweet-talks them. I hear he's got them working three shifts making bush beer for him . . ." Farniff stiffens, cradling his earphones closer. "This poor bastard's got troubles."

Arnold steps over, listens, then take Farniff's place. While Farniff cranks the field phone to alert Direction Finding, Arnold hears a radio operator somewhere in the night skies nearby pounding out his distress in clear English: *Me lost rpt lost where am I.*

There is a Japanese tape wheel going at the same time, from a souped-up transmitter in the Marshall Islands: *Qra Qra Qra de Jap Jap Jap QTC imi Tu Pse.* The name of my station is J.A.P. Have you any traffic for me? Thank you, please.

Neither one will quit. The Jap wheel keeps revolving in its endless idiot catechism, expecting no answer and listening for none, simply creating whatever interference it can for operators too inexperienced to copy through it. The American has his fist frozen to the key in a blind, unhearing panic. He doesn't even think of switching to another frequency. Or maybe he hasn't time to. Maybe that ocean is coming toward him sickeningly fast.

Easy, boy, Arnold murmurs, stop just a second. Listen, will you? I'm *here*, for Christ's sake. He taps the key, sending steady-spaced dashes; trying to cut through, to insinuate his presence somehow. He prints his call letters on the deaf sky. Now Farniff shoves him a slip of paper. It has a compass heading on it: D.F. has found the ship. If Arnold can get the magic numbers across, it will turn its nose in some new direction, the six, ten, twenty men aboard will sit back in relief, and in perhaps an hour they'll be close enough to hear the voice of Rocky Base tower.

SOS SOS SOS.

Thank you, please.

The American gives up. He has screwed his key shut, making it transmit one continuous dash to mark his position, in case Air-Sea Rescue cares to pick up the pieces. The long dash whines eerily in Arnold's earphones, like a rapidly descending motor.

Then he realizes the air raid siren is going, rising and falling in the flood-lit night.

He wrenches the earphones free and slams them to

the floor. "You ignorant son of a bitch, will you *listen?*"
Cady is stunned. "They weren't bluffing, then."

In embarrassment, Arnold picks up the earphones as
Farniff says irritably, "It's just a coincidence. One
outfit runs the war, another runs the propaganda. They
don't co-ordinate these things any better than us." He
looks questioningly at Arnold.

"I lost him," Arnold says. "Go ahead, take off. I'll
shut down."

As they head for the foxhole he puts out the Condition Red on all circuits, to warn off any inbound
traffic. Then he turns off the transmitters so the raiders
will have nothing to home on. A mere formality; they'll
find their way.

"What's this war all about?" Little Orphan Annie
is asking in feminine confusion. "Maybe I'm stupid,
but I can't see what all the fighting's for . . ."

Stumbling at the edge of the runway, Arnold drops
to one knee on the spongy coral. He brushes himself
off and jogs into the patchy undergrowth. Through
the shaggy ferns and sweetly rotten vegetation, palm
trees stand like mired masts. The hole is just behind
the airplane revetments, substantial beneath its logs
and layered sandbags. He stands at the edge for a moment, listening. There is no sound. The atoll waits
nakedly beneath the hot moon. He eases himself into
the earth.

Even here there is dank heat, doubled by the breath
of Farniff and Cady. Their faces take shape behind

cupped cigarettes. Cady's fatigues have a fresh glazed smell.

"Do they usually take this long to get here, Sergeant?" he asks.

"No idea, Cady. We're all virgins together."

"But Sergeant Levine said . . ." He lowers his voice to keep Farniff from hearing. "He said if anything happened, could he have the rest of my subscription to *Time*."

Arnold tries not to smile. "We're non-combat personnel, Cady. Our only enemy is ptomaine poisoning."

"Suppose it's just another false alarm?" Farniff asks.

"Probably not. They want those Baker 24's."

Damn good thing they are out on a strike. All that the raiders will find here will be a few cripples, which they can break into spare parts as easily as the squadron mechs. The Seabees will have their work cut out for them, repairing the runway in time for the strikers' return.

"But when they don't find anything," Cady insists, "maybe they'll go on up the line—or even turn back?"

"Maybe. I doubt it."

A twig snaps and all three jump.

"At ease, soldiers!" Ben Levine's double chins appear at the opposite opening. He has on a conical reed hat that some native wove for him in exchange for a G.I. undershirt. "Is this the limited-servicemen's hole?" He squeezes in heavily. "Hey, filter center says they're forty miles out. The whole screen's full of bogies."

"I sure wish we'd built this thing *deep*," Farniff
mutters.

"Now he talks deep," Ben says in gloomy relish.
"Was I against it deep?"

"I never noticed you on any digging detail, buddy."

"I got in my licks, buddy. You should've been here
when it was rough."

Routed, Farniff says, "What's the gas mask for, Levine? Going to war or something?"

"This here's my scrounge bag. I been shopping."
Ben opens the pack of his gas mask to give them a
glimpse of selected rations. "Siren him cry, mess sergeant him go bush, all same big fella bird. No lock 'im
door. Me stop longside plenty good fella kai-kai." He
crawls over to Arnold, slips something in his pocket.
"Keep it to yourself. I only got a couple."

Arnold lights a match, screening it from the opening.
"Oh, those pigs," he says, "those lousy *pigs*." He blows
out the match (knowing Ben is grinning) and sits
back feeling not hate anymore, but only weary contempt. He is used to buying cigarettes at the PX
stamped "Gift to our armed forces overseas." He is
used to drawing three cans of beer a week when his
allotment is seven. He is used to so much that he
should be used to this little can that Ben has stolen
for him, or rather, repossessed. It is a standard army
ration, in regulation drab lacquer, but he has never
heard of its existence. Like the cigarette graft, the
chiseled beer, the shipments of fresh meat or eggs or

books, it has gone directly into Officers' Country. It
contains boned turkey.

"Now that I know it's around," Ben says, "I can make
a deal with the mess officer."

Arnold has to smile. "You marvelous bastard. How
much money do you make a month?"

"About twice what you do. I could still use a partner.
It's clean, I don't gyp my buddies."

"I know you don't," Arnold admits. "I'm just not interested in making a career out of the goddamn war."

Ben stares at him in baffled anger. Suddenly the
anti-aircraft batteries let loose.

All over the island the big rifles begin coughing from
their emplacements, the shells thudding with the sound
and frequency of a man kicking footballs, one after the
other. The sky beyond the foxhole cracks open, letting
sheets of daylight through. And now comes the grad-
ual high-pitched drone of motors, like the sound of
mosquitoes through a dream of drowning. Other motors
begin warming up and, incredulous, Arnold realizes it
is a couple of marine pilots, with their sheer brass guts,
going up in the pair of clumsy F4U's, trying to make
night fighters out of submarine spotters. Do they think
they can get above the raiders and drop depth bombs
on them?

Ben has to lean close to make himself heard. "What's
so different about war? You don't like officers? I like
them fine. They're smart, they don't let moss grow
under their prats. They'll go home with a B bag full

of gold. Don't be so big a putz, Arnold. Wise up, this is the world!"

There is a new commotion. "Look, they're catching one!"

Arnold kneels cautiously in the opening to watch. A twin-engined Mitsubishi is lit by one searchlight, grazed by another, then trapped in the cross-beams. It lies stationary in the moving lights, like an impaled silver moth, huge with eggs. A stream of tracers rises, seeming to curve far short of it. It hangs untouched for an unbearable interval. The searchlights leisurely follow the congealed twistings of its evasive action, then just as leisurely lose it back to the rushing darkness. The men curse the gunners bitterly.

The Japs are pissed-off at the empty runway, Arnold thinks, smothering a wild impulse to laugh. Maybe they'll drop fraction bars instead of bombs.

As the first demolition bomb crunches on the far side of the airstrip, he scrambles back into the hole. The bombers are peeling off on their first pass, sowing five-hundred pounders in pairs. Each man measures the interval between concussions, as the pattern is walked gigantically across the runway toward them. An airplane erupts into bits in the near revetment.

Arnold thinks fleetingly of the natives, who would be hiding beneath their overturned canoes in the lagoon, from some insane atavism. And then his sympathy turns to bile. They're home, this is where they lead their lives. They can die here, and they'll only be out more of the same . . . A wide loneliness permeates

him. What will become of him if he is smeared into
the earth? Only his dogtags will remain, slim proof
that he ever existed. Don't think about it. Don't think
of anything except its being over and you in the sack
opening that can of turkey turkey turkey . . .

An ammunition dump blows off like a midget earthquake. There is the sound of a dozen waterfalls briefly
in the air, exhausting itself. Forty-five belts are pop-
ping in scattered clusters from the ignited cartons.

"Mamma mia!" Ben says. "Where's my white flag?"

And now they freeze, hearing a sound they haven't
heard before. It is the delicate fluting of air through
the fins of a bomb, dropping directly overhead. It falls
and falls forever, and in its whistle, Arnold hears the
message that he is a dead man.

Jeeeeeee-SUS!

Dirt showers down on him, filling his collar. He is
deafened, till he hears himself begin to breathe again.
He opens his eyes. Cady is holding a cigarette, looking
as if he wants to get it to his mouth but has forgotten
the muscles that are involved.

"Oh," he says. "Oh. Oh. Oh."

Arnold slips the can of boned turkey into Cady's free
hand and folds his limp fingers around it. The batteries
begin quieting. The first wave is over.

As the F4U's come back to land, a sprinkling of small
arms fire is directed at them from the marine emplacements. Arnold puts his arms around his knees, rolls
himself up like a fetus, and waits in the warm darkness
to be born. In the instant that he shuts his eyes, he

sees Ben gently remove the can of turkey from Cady's fingers, not disturbing him at all.

Meanwhile, because he has not died, Arnold undergoes gestation, rising through the millenia that lie ahead till he can be reborn, poor fish of a statistic, as a free and naked individual awaiting cloth of his own cutting. He swears a solemn oath that on the day of discharge he will be his own man. Life, he knows now, is too short for hypocrisy or compromise, for humiliation of any kind after this total humiliation. And as the dreamer dreams of his integrity, he is wrapped in the music of a dying airman's swan song and the laughter of Levine and Annie.

The millennia have passed. Fled is that music: does he wake or sleep?

MEXICAN
HÁYRIDE

*N*ight lay over Lake Chapala with the permanence
of settled ruins. There were no sounds to it, no future.
Creased shadows in the hills denied the moon to certain tilted cornfields, bared others to the granite evening. It could have been the San Francisco headlands,
and Warner waited for the fog's far harbingers: its
first deep diaphones speaking profoundly from Point
Bonita to Mile Rock to Lime Point to the great orange
bridge itself, then all the littler heralds urging the
alarm, hooting from shelf to ship to inlet to pier as
startled gulls revolved above the rocking buoys . . . But
the only tumult was the mush and oscillation of his own

[185]

mortality, auricle to ventricle; the only gulls the buzzards in their sere roosts, who by day considered him and took the long view. Now the sky began widening with wind. A night bird entered, whistling up its dinner or its mate. Whistling in echo, but not expecting anything of it, Warner took the cobbled climb from shore.

Farmers and their families were dropping off the buses from outlying villages, setting up their sidewalk emporiums (no taxes, no overhead, out of the high-rent district). Avocados stacked in fives, unchanged since the Tarascan bazaars, a peso a pyramid; melons fresh from the vine, and scallions clotted with warm earth. The movie had already started, the late arrivees hurrying inside with their chairs. The programs were made up of newsreels, interspliced with a U.S. Western featuring stars long resident in Forest Lawn, but young and fearless here forever. There were occasional Spanish subtitles. Those who could read repeated them in unison for those who couldn't. Now and then the cinema folk would do something immoral or incomprehensible or simply dull, and the Mexicans would whistle severely, the way one does at a bull ring when the matadors refuse to earn their handsome fees. It seemed to have little effect. Warner's countrymen would soon be gathering for canasta or charades, followed by loud, bad Bach and bad, flat highballs. It was Sunday. But then it's always Sunday in the American colony.

He cut up toward the Spring of Grace. Women were

grouped around it balancing water jugs, their strong hips braced against the weight and seeming continuous with their lesser vessels. A pack train of firewood came jogging through the dusk. The burros passed him with forlorn, liquid eyes, like backslid deer in an evil incarnation. Across the street stood a Packard, six years older than it was when it arrived here, but still serviceable. Ask the lady who owns one. The lady was also six years older and could stand it less.

Her house was dark, her door agape, as always. Her dog leaped on Warner in the shadowed hallway, whining with delight and bumping its clumsy butt against him. Warner cuffed it on the snout, and assuming he was playing it fell into a fit of capering and barking.

"Now, Puppyduckles, quit that ruckus," a sugary voice from inside sang; then: "*Quiénnn?*"

"Only us chickens," Warner called, coming up into the patio.

On the rope bed that doubled as a couch he made out the forms of Victory Richmond and Dionisio Gómez, bundled under a serape. They brought their hands out from beneath—Victory a little self-consciously as she sat forward to light the lamp.

"Well, Warner, I haven't seen you in a month of Sundays."

"How's ever little thang, Miss Victory? *Qué tal, hombre?*" He nodded to Dionisio.

"*Q'hubo*, Huarner?" Dionisio answered lazily.

"My, I didn't have the least idea it was so dark. I

expect one's eyes get accustomed. We were just sitting here discussing a chair Dionisio's mending for me."

"He's quite a mender," Warner said, taking a cowhide chair opposite them. There was a silence. "Clever with his hands," he claimed.

"Yes, well, and then you know how these things go in Spanish." Victory fanned herself with a magazine. "The time it can consume."

"You mean it takes longer in Spanish? I always heard it was the other way around."

She managed to look maligned. "I don't believe I care for your insinuations, Warner."

"Was I insinuating again? God dammit, I'll never learn to speak directly."

"That's a very definite trait in your character, I've noticed. Suspicion."

He winked at her deliberately. She struggled to remain slurred Southern womanhood, then gave up, laughing.

"Contrary to what you're thinking, I don't spend *all* my time that way."

Quite an attractive lady, this Mrs. Richmond, Warner thought. Rather eerily so, because before too much longer she'd be half a century old. She had one of those lucky complexions that would last as long as she would, plus sensibly cut blond hair and a durable figure from which she wrung the liquor calories by fanatic afternoons of ping-pong. But it was mostly love and laughter, equally unmotivated, that kept her supple.

"Care for a Pepsi, Warner?" When Victory was on the wagon, everyone was on the wagon.

"No, thanks." He was too lazy to get one from the icebox.

"There's a fresh lemonade if you'd prefer. The pitcher's over yonder."

"That's a thought. Got any rum to cut it with?"

"The maid hid it."

"Where?"

"How should I know?"

"I mean, got any ideas?"

She was only politely concerned. "No telling how her mind connives. Reckon you should try the well?"

"The well?" Warner hiked over to it, pulled the bucket up. A wicker jug of rum was nestled in it. A clear case of clairvoyance. It turned out that Victory would also have a little dash of rum, just a smidgen, in her lemonade. Dionisio had his straight.

Absently lowering half her glass, Victory said, "How's your play progressing, Warner?"

"I ought to finish up this scene I'm on next month."

"Isn't that just grand?"

Now it was his turn. "How's the sculpting coming?"

"Well, ordinarily wild horses couldn't drag me from it. But I've had to wear myself to the bone with *this* one," she jabbed an elbow in Dionisio's ribs, "getting him to comprehend the *simplest* work I want done. Honestly, if I waited for him to exercise the least scrap of initiative I'd be dead and buried. Warner, honey, would you float a teeny weeny bit of rum on top of this? It's awfully concentrated lemonade."

Bored by all the English, Dionisio picked up the guitar he'd sold Victory and was theoretically teaching her. He began singing in the pleasant near-falsetto that, in Mexico as well as Ireland, every male seemed born with.

> *Arroz con leche/Me quiero casar*
> *Con una muñeca/De este lugar.* . . .

The village waxed and waned with the lake, and in the dissolutely handsome face of Dionisio Gómez you could read its present level. If it were higher, permitting fishing and swimming, there would be a flood of tourists with chairs requiring mending and occasions requiring streetsingers. The merchants would prosper, and Dionisio would be carpentering by day and working the fiestas by night, growing fat and dull and moral. His wife could buy material for twenty dresses if she liked, his children could have toys in abundance. And as for his mistress, she would be a *muñeca* of this locality (as he was singing), shy and unhandled, and speaking only when she was addressed, instead of this witless pampered whore (as he would put it) who spoke no sense continuously in a barbaric tongue, and from whom he was forced to accept money which, though he more than earned it, was a reflection on his integrity and could only be assuaged by quantities of her rum, which only made him sullen.

Qué te parece, hombre?" Warner asked him. "Will the lake regain its height someday?"

"Why not?" Dionisio said irritably. "If this cuckolding drought abates and there be rains. Provided that your countrymen devise no bigger bombs to change the weather."

"I'll write my senator," Warner told him.

He smiled sourly and shifted into a brisk canteen tune. He played as well as he ever would, since it was beneath a musician's dignity to practice once he got to be a *maestro.*

"O-*lay!*" Victory clapped her hands. "Isn't he just heavenly? It's that Spanish blood, it'll tell every time. If only he didn't incline to drink so heavily." She rumpled his hair reprovingly.

"What is this that she says now?" he asked Warner.

"That you are number one of the guitar."

He grunted. "Your brains come in bottles," he told her, and pointed at the rum jug. "Educate yourself!"

But she was busy studying the flat planes of his face. "If he isn't the *spit*-image of some old Toltec idol. I'm simply going to *have* to do a bust of him."

Warner helped himself to another few inches of rum. Dionisio was puzzling out the melody line of something, getting as far as the fifth bar when he'd bog down each time. Victory sighed.

"They're just like children, aren't they? Not a solitary grief in all creation. The church baptizes them and the church buries them, and in between it does their thinking." She grabbed Dionisio's hair and shook his head. "Don't you want to *make* something of yourself? Don't you want to go back to America with me and get on television?"

He ignored her.

"Just like talking to a stone wall. Look," she told him, "*oo-sted*," she jabbed him in the chest, "*yo*," she prodded her hospitable bosom, "*el Estados Oo-nidos? Mucho dinero?*"

"*Como quiera Diós*," he said dryly. As God wishes.

"There, you see?" Victory said in sad triumph. "I'd give anything if I could have their simple faith. Oh, well, I don't care to trouble myself about the hereafter." With the rum beginning to reach her, she turned moody. "I'm a fatalist. There's no way of changing what's to come. Let's live a while before we have to pay for it."

There was a clatter of feet in the hallway, and Cassius came running in. The dog sprang up, tackling him halfway, and after wrestling with it briefly he broke loose. Thwarted, it doubled back and leaped into Warner's chair. He smacked it heavily in the side and it fell down, wagging its tail and barking frenziedly.

"Now, Warner, don't encourage her," Victory said. "If she gets too excited she makes doo-doo on the mats. Well, young man, it's high time you were coming in for supper."

Cass came on up, panting. He greeted Warner as coolly as he dared with his ten years. Then he edged over to the table and glanced in Victory's glass casually.

"We were taking a little lemonade for refreshment," she said quickly. "There's more in the pitcher."

He picked up her glass and sniffed it.

She took it from him with a silvery laugh. "You don't want this, dear. I let Warner put a little rum on top to be sociable."

"Better lay off it," Cass said.

"Why, what on earth—I'm *ashamed* I heard you say that," Victory said. "Just what was the nature of that innuendo, pray?"

The boy turned away in defeat. "Listen, I got to have two pesos. I need a tablet for school."

"You do, do you?" she said. "Well, it may interest you to know I'm not putting out one red cent more for tablets. I'll give you the opportunity to speak straightforward. What happened to the one I gave you money for last week?"

Cass was trapped. "Chuey's goat ate it."

Victory laughed, the perspective restored once more between indulgent mother and transparent child.

"How can you keep ahead of them?" she told Warner. "All right, run ask Alberta where my purse is, and tell her to fix you and Warner a plate of whatever's in the oven."

Warner went through the motions of refusing his only meal since breakfast, but to no avail. Back from the kitchen, Cass shyly settled himself at the feet of Dionisio, whom he placed in a stabler category than his mother's other gentlemen callers.

"What must a man do, Dionisio, if insulted by a stronger man?"

"*Pos*, Cass, no man is as strong as the edge of a knife."

"Yes, but I am not yet a man."

"Someone gave you insult?"

"To me, no. To my mother."

"An insult of what nature?"

"That she was a woman of moral irresponsibility, liberal with her body."

"Who said this?"

"The nephew of Eliseo of the goats."

"The fat one with the cockeye?"

"No, the tall one of the measle scars."

"I will speak to Eliseo. There will be no more of this."

"Your word?"

"My word. . . ."

Self-consciously, Warner picked up one of Cass's comic books. Soon he was a gullible tourist in a realm where a mouse named El Ratón Miguelito was the owner of a foolish, talking dog, and a duck known as Pato Pascual went fox hunting. At the bottom of each page there would be inspirational slogans. *Save: you gain and Mexico progresses. Prefer the book that educates, not the alcohol that debases.*

Now Alberta brought their plates in, and Cass kept her running for fresh tortillas. They made pretty fair *tacos* when the canned pork and beans were rolled in them. They also had pork chops, a little burnt, but more free from trichinosis that way. Cass was talking and waving a taco, and it dribbled on him.

"Cassie, dear, I *wish* you could learn to cultivate a few graces at the table," Victory said. "You're getting to be as bad as the Mexicans."

He nodded absently, finished bolting his food and cut for the door.

"Cassius! You're not to leave the house this evening, you hear? You're keeping entirely too late hours, you need the sleep for school."

"I'll be right back," he called. "We got a calf cornered down at Lalo's barn and I have to fight it." And he was gone.

Victory sighed, reaching for the rum. "Sometimes I just can't fathom that child's attitude. Be a lamb, Warner, and fetch the lemonade?"

By the time he got back out on the street, Jesús Ochoa was getting ready to crank down the Virgin-blue riot door of his grocery shop named The Eternal Struggle. A short fat man of military leanings, armed with a mustache like Zapata's, he was scowling hideously at the prosperity of his adjacent competitor, The Sun Shines For All. His vegetables were deployed in tidy ranks, like the bric-à-brac retired colonels use to reconstruct old battles.

"Yes, sir," Warner said. "Another day, another dollar."

Jesús smiled blankly. "*Mande?*"

"No importance. How is the señora?"

"Well, thanks."

"And the children?"

"Also. Without novelty. And yourself?"

"Equally. And the crops?"

Jesús shrugged. "Average, no more."

"And the midnight crop?" Warner asked delicately.

Jesús assumed a guarded expression. Cautiously, he removed a packet from a locked drawer. Fifty grams' worth. They settled on a price of two pesos, which was put on Warner's tab, along with half a liter of cane alcohol. Partway back to Doña Felipa's, the lights went out all over town. Lightning in the mountains, maybe, or just some truck colliding with a pole. Warner eased his way through the extinguished streets, beneath a wind-driven moon, to the *posada* door; felt out the bell rope and leaned on it. After a while the old girl slapped on down to let him in, her lantern shedding a waxen path back to the patio.

From its trellis the *teléfono* vine, the width of Warner's finger, sprawled like a stunned snake, its dark green leaves glistening richly as a pelt. Growing from a deceptively small pot, like a cobra from a basket, it lay in a digestive stupor. Almost half as old as himself, it was, like himself, a carnivore. Doña Felipa treated it regularly to saucers of blood, on which it thrived and fattened and waited through the hungry evenings, its thousand pointed leaves thrust out like tongues.

The doña raised her lantern. Shall I make a little omelet for you, Señor Huarner?" she asked hopefully.

"Thanks, no. I have already eaten."

She left him to the shadows, pleased at having just the one meal on his day's bill. Miz Richmond's im-

ported pork-and-beans were still a gluey filler in his
stomach, and he wondered if the *teléfono* vine had
done as well. They considered one another in the rust-
ling night. What was it that cannibals called fillet of
human? Long pig. Care for a spot of Dr. Livingston's
Long Pork and Beans, you bastard? Next time I cut
myself shaving I'll give you a break.

Then, dialing the combination lock, Warner let himself into the door of his home and castle.

It was composed of one large room, with adobe
walls unadorned except by whitewash. There were no
pinups, pots of sweet peas, conversation pieces. Instead, he had four blank screens for the projection of
whatever whimsies or horrors he was given by euphoria,
either self-induced or chemically assisted. There was a
table with a typewriter, a shelf of books, a chair, ash
trays, et cetera, and upstage left a bed, for the develop-
ment of the Freudian underlife.

Now he took his half quart of pure cane alcohol,
one hundred ninety proof, and mixed it with half a
quart of reasonably pure water. This gave him one full
quart of ninety-five-proof white rum, otherwise known
as Old Doc Warner's Sunday Punch. Next he carefully shook out the packet Jesús had given him. The
stuff was unworked, just as it came stripped from the
plant. There were seeds with it, about the size of bar-
ley, and pieces of stem; but it was mostly dried and
crumbled leaves, olive drab, somewhat resembling
orégano. A little more piquant, however. By a process
of tilting and scraping it the heavier impurities were

separated, and he ended up with a tiny mound of powder known to all good Fagins variously as tea, jive, pot, hay, hemp, Maryjane.

Rolling himself a stick of it, Warner lit up and drew a lungful, along with some air for carburetion. He held it as long as he could, gradually exhaled, seeing his streaked breath in the candlelight; got that metallic aftertaste, shuddered, coughed and lit a natural cigarette. Three drags later and the chore was done, the psyche cast adrift. For the next odd ninety minutes he would be someone else's creature.

He wound the clock, reality's compass, and arbitrarily set it for midnight. He would be free at one-thirty. But if the clock stopped, he was done for; there'd be no way of ever getting back.

The lights came back on, the sudden glare jarring him. He snapped them off, poured a shot of alcohol to set the marijuana, and with the smell of burnt weeds in the air he settled back to wait for news from Shangri-la.

It wasn't long in coming. First, from far away, there was the sound of the sea in his ears, the way you'd hear it through a faulty sea shell. Then this sea gently tugged at his extremities, cooling them and causing them to tingle. The tide rose, gathering and carrying him, and he was lifted from his chair to stand enormous in its seething center, clearheaded, bared and buoyant.

Then in that ever new and startling way, the shift set in. Perspective warped, so imperceptibly that it

could only be detected sideways. Contours were sof-
tened, but in no way blurred. And now a great inner
organ of perception opened, like the engaging of an
unused brain lobe. Through it, Warner became
minutely aware of himself, the branching of the capil-
lary system, the breathing of the pores, the hustling
ganglia and the old persistent heart, revving like a
stone engine. He monitored these activities for quite
some time (directing them, in fact) in awe and wonder. He expanded with self-appreciation. God *damn*,
he thought, this is *some* hay.

Suddenly everything was funny. The way the chair
sat at such a ludicrous angle to the floor, the silly-assed
candle consuming itself, and his drunken, grotesque
self. His stomach worked in convulsive spasms of
laughter. Then quite abruptly, he was sober.

Warner picked up the clock. It was five past midnight.

He sat down, emptied of any emotion whatsoever,
waiting for something he couldn't quite remember—
and then it started up again, beginning to lift him on
a new and higher wave. He hurried to the typewriter,
wanting to be ready when it broke. It took the damned-
est time to get a sheet of paper in the machine. His
hands were uncoordinated, like a spastic's; he was way
ahead of his body.

Finally Warner groped open his play folder, with its
scribbled notes on characters, the half-assembled
scenes, the clever exits and the midnight flashes. Ignoring all external trivia, such as the interpenetration of

his fingers with the space bar, he began to put it all down. There were no doubts now, no reservations. He saw his entire play, from the opening curtain to the last slow close, the action vivid and convincing, the people bursting with life. But the mechanics of translating it to paper kept getting in the way. Each word that leaped to print swarmed with rich new vistas of association, and the exploration of them was compulsive. Simultaneously, there was a canny campaign taking place to resist this compulsion, to smuggle out the message.

Come on, fool, say it. It's never been so comprehensible. Indispensable. Consequenceable, evidenceable, uncondensable—uncondensable? Now, really, Warner, what kind of woolly terminology is this? Why, it's beautiful terminology, so I guess you can go poop, Warner. Poop, is it? Just for that I guess you can have a knee in the brisket.

Gradually, a mellow lassitude invaded him, pinning his arms to the table. He'd make it yet, if not tonight some other night. He couldn't miss . . .

He came back to himself with the feel of boulders being rolled from his chest. His heart was jumping like a rabbit in a sack. He could move again. We've been away for quite a while, haven't we? Next time leave a forwarding address.

The clock read 12:22.

He picked it up in a panic of disbelief, shook it. He'd been completely loaded, *stoned*, for at least one full hour. He *knew* it had been at least an hour. That meant he couldn't trust himself because he was only twenty-two minutes along, with the peak yet to come. At that rate it might be hours—days even, before he got in phase with time again. *Maybe never*, a voice chuckled in his skull. After all, it's called loco weed, isn't it? You poor son of a bitch, you've skewed yourself into insanity and you'll never make it back.

Warner sat in quiet terror, up to the forehead, those delicate prefrontal lobes with their fused synapses, in a pool of ice water. Nothing significant in itself had changed. He was aware of shapes and objects, but there was just a terribly thin screen between them and himself.

Then, while he waited in the void, he realized that it was 12:23.

All the filaments of his body brimmed with relief as he watched the clock hand moving, the slow wheel ferrying him home. Only an hour more to go. He'd make it, no matter how long it took. Pushing aside the folder entitled *Six Authors In Search of a Character*, he decided this wasn't his night. Instead, he began another letter to the girl he used to introduce to people as his first wife.

Dear Gerry:
I made a little poem for you, a nonheroic couplet.
                          G
                          Me
No period, because it never stops.
Remember Russian Hill in San Francisco, in the rain, the

bay full of foghorns and the air with bells? And you, adrift on the up-anchored night beside me, while the lisping rain communicated with the roofs. From the window I could see two muffled stars, enough to steer by. Fresh from the fevered country of your hair, I'd watch your body curving to the mattress's polarity. You slept, the rain's casual syllables went past; while I, child of short memory in the banished wood, would search your pollen-heavy lids and that herbed mouth loose from love's small language, for the warm way back. And now my love the angel bitch, my first and last wife Oh she sleeps in other climates now oh now is the time for all good alienists to come to the aid of a wandering client who can't lie still for long enough to get a Junging, Ranking, Reiking, and most especially a thorough Berglerizing and be robbed of all necessity to be himself . . .

He cradled his head on the typewriter. It made a Gerry-cold lap for him, and he must have slept a little. Eventually it was 1:30, as it had to be, and he was out of it.

He reached for the lights, but they were off again. As his hand paused above the dwindling candle Warner could see his wrist vein throbbing, and for the first time in his life he understood that some day, between two pulses, it would stop. And now he knew that Victory Richmond understood all this, and more. For once she was dead, she'd have to go to hell.

His pulse picked up its canter, merged with the rhythm of the nightly herd of wild burros as they came galloping down the cobbles, their breaths whuffing in the stone-rung evening. The candle bluttered.

I wish I could tell Victory it's not so bad in hell, he thought. *At times it's really not so bad at all.*